The History of America in My Lifetime

Brooks Sterritt

SPUYTEN DUYVIL
New York City

ISBN 978-1-952419-04-1

Library of Congress Cataloging-in-Publication Data

Names: Sterritt, Brooks, author.
Title: The history of America in my lifetime / Brooks Sterritt.
Description: New York : Spuyten Duyvil, [2021] |
Identifiers: LCCN 2021001000 | ISBN 9781952419041 (paperback)
Subjects: LCSH: Sterritt, Brooks--Fiction. | GSAFD: Autobiographical
fiction.
Classification: LCC PS3619.T4787447 H57 2021 | DDC 813/.6--dc23
LC record available at https://lccn.loc.gov/2021001000

Pseudepigraphical Material

Sex	*Male*
Name	*[redacted]*
Age	*30*
Height	*5'11" (claims six feet)*
Weight	*136-171 pounds*
Character	*Obsessive*
Discipline	*Sloppy*
Associates	*None*

WHAT FOLLOWS IS AN ACCOUNT of events experienced
by the above man. As a film subject, he was one of the best
I've ever seen, despite a complete lack of dramatic ability.
The sources I've used for the creation of this report are, in
the main, video footage—both consensual interviews with
the subject and footage generated without his knowledge.
At the time of this writing, he is employed at a facility
called Shred Authority Neighborhood Storage. In terms
of familial relationships, he has two sisters (no contact), a
mother (no contact), and a father (yearly contact). His sexual
interests are best described as disappointingly vanilla
with longtime urges for mild deviancy. Hobbies include
cycling, occasional woodworking, and researching arcane
topics on the Internet and internalizing them. He lacks
a formal education, yet is adept at finding information,
albeit in an unsystematic way. I chose this subject not
because of the events he experienced—though they are
thrilling and profound—but because he stumbled across
something that no one could turn away from. Though a
select few of you may be familiar with my film work, I've
recently retired to pursue other forms, hence the at times
novelistic appearance of the following narrative.

—Lucian Bevacqua, Auteur, Founder of
the Global Institute of Film and Fragmentation

1

On the day of the encounter I was returning from a conference organized by the Supranational Association for Information Destruction (SAID). My employer, a document storage and shredding facility, had insisted I attend.

While waiting to board my flight home, I noticed a figure sitting in the gate's crowded waiting area. What first drew my eye was the space around the man—despite the number of travelers standing, leaning, sitting in bolted-down chairs and on the floor, vacant seats flanked him on either side. I watched the mother in line ahead of me snatch a look, her hand resting on her small son's head.

I looked again and couldn't look away. What I saw could lead to one of three conclusions: something was wrong with my eyes, something was amiss with the stranger's face, or something had transpired between my eyes and his face to cause the distortion I was seeing. The stranger's face could only be called pixelated. His face and the space around it was a blur, obscured by rippling pixel-like squares. I glanced at other nearby faces, but the distortion was limited to this solitary figure. I did what you do when your vision is in question: rubbed my eyes, squeezed them shut, blinked frenetically. The figure remained, cloaked in blur.

I began to experience actual fear.

The mother and son in front of me were now the next to board. The boy fidgeted, rotating his upper body and swinging his arms while his mother handed over the tickets. As I stepped forward, the ticket agent turned to the seating area, raising his voice to single out the figure.

"Are you able to board now, sir?" he said.

The figure rose and began to shuffle over, the blur moving with him. He wore a dark suit and tie, with a long black wool coat over everything. The ticket agent took my boarding pass while the stranger approached at a painfully slow rate. I entered the jetway, hoping for the largest possible buffer between us. One line became another and I tried to smile each time the mother in front of me glanced anxiously back.

Baggage handlers formed a stopgap at the jetway's end, taking bags too large to be carried on. I hurried onto the plane as I heard a handler ask the figure behind me if he was traveling or going home—he said he was going home. The man sounded like a relative of mine at the end of his life, post-tracheotomy. His voice also brought to mind the distorted, slowed down voices of interviewees who wished to remain anonymous.

I took my seat, an aisle blocking two empty spots, and felt dread build at the prospect of sitting next to the stranger for the duration of the flight. I rehearsed what I would say should his seat be next to mine, picturing my eventual nonchalant and friendly behavior and planning conversation points. My behavior would be so casual, so genuine, that he would be bowled over by my goodwill. I congratulated myself in advance and swallowed hard when he appeared in the aisle.

The area around the stranger's face undulated, was impossible to hold in view for long. I've since learned that this effect is called "fogging," or "tiling" in television and film. One couldn't help but think of the reality TV series involving law enforcement in which the faces of perpetrators were often blurred, or any number of true crime shows featuring surveillance footage. With a glance, I tried to take in the floating flesh-colored squares that obscured his head and shoulder region. Struggling for something fixed, my eyes settled on a black lapel pin featuring a symbol: a little letter.

a

The longer I stared at the lapel pin, the less certain I became that the symbol engraved there was actually a letter. I wasn't sure it was even a symbol. Was it merely a circle next to a vertical line? Was it nothing more than a shape?

"Are you in this row, sir?" I managed to ask.

The figure froze and all sound on the plane seemed to cease. His lapel pin grew into a black archery target in my awareness, until he made a noise and shuffled off. I leaned my head back and opened the air valve above me, which didn't function. I looked across the aisle at a woman calmly holding a book whose spine read "GOYA." She didn't behave as if she'd seen what I had seen, if I had seen anything at all.

I felt the allure of a simple explanation: what I saw was an illusion, a hallucination, a trick of the light, a figment, a blip. The human brain and eye are our most fallible organs. We misremember, fill in details, construct them, leave ourselves open to suggestion. Another soothing explanation involved a new, possibly experimental technology. I had read of ways to confuse facial recognition software, usually through makeup, prosthetics, and masks. If a recognition algorithm backed by a database could be fooled, why not the human visual apparatus?

A man spoke to me, reaching to tap my shoulder but not quite touching it. I stood to let him into the center seat. He commented how full the flight was after settling in. It was a relief to be distracted, if only on the surface. Neither one of us stood when someone came for the window seat.

I decreased the brightness of my seat's screen until it went dark. The man next to me was absorbed in a magazine. I wondered where the figure was sitting, imagined him, face blanked out, surrounded by empty seats: three in the row in front, three behind, and one to either side.

I regretted skipping a visit to the airport terminal restroom. The flight was short, and if I didn't get up soon I'd have to wait until landing. Despite my urgent need, I didn't want to venture into the rear of the plane. I rose and took in the field of screens in headrests. Three in a row featured an unkempt Nicolas Cage on an aircraft, and I imagined a scenario in which all of the plane's screens displayed airborne cinematic content: hostage situations, chance meetings, romantic encounters, tales of air travel as disease vector, aviophobia narratives, military sorties, airline industry exposés, natural disasters, sagas of hotshot pilotage, solo feats of aviation, in-flight trysts, jaded business traveler yarns, ill-fated crashes, bereaved pilgrimages, disturbing window views, tales of separation anxiety, survivor guilt, terrorism, snakes, titillation on the wing.

Against my better judgment, I scanned passenger faces before entering a bathroom next to the cockpit. Inside, I couldn't stand without various body parts encountering the walls. On the subway I try to lean, rather than touch straps or bars with my hands. I remembered reading that a large percentage of any given human is actually other organisms, but I could never bring myself to try to confirm the claim.

I looked down at the blue stuff in the metal bowl, thought about what must fill the plane's tank. An aircraft like this one can hold 150 gallons of waste (85 in the forward tank, 65 in the aft), a solid/liquid mixture. I used to think planes dumped their tanks at 30,000 feet, counting on sufficient dispersal of the waste due to extreme height.

The seatbelt sound dinged in the small space and the plane started to go down. I made my way back to my seat and was relieved when every face I encountered was of normal composition—no vortices or wavelets. The man in my row ("our" row, as I came to think of it) made small talk. He told me his occupation and name, which I nearly immediately forgot.

It was difficult to say which was stronger: my earlier desire to enter the plane or my urge to leave upon landing. I had nevertheless almost convinced myself the stranger was a figment, a flashback, a neurological burp.

They were connecting the jetway. I needed to wash my hands in the terminal. The cabin bathroom is no use because if they only have hand sanitizer, there remains a lock to unlock after your hands are sterile. If there is soap, you have to touch something to dispense it, the water faucet leaves you with a dirty hand if you have to touch it to turn it off, and one touch on a delayed water release system is never enough to rinse off all the soap, so you end up touching the tap with a clean hand, which many others have done before you. Oddly enough, I never really minded camping.

Passengers spilled out. Nearly free, I reached an elderly fellow rummaging in the overhead bin and pulled his bag down for him. To be helpful, to feel good, but mostly to hasten my exit. I passed the terminal's first available men's room because I knew others would flock to it, and I especially wanted to avoid coming face-to-face, so to speak, with the stranger again.

I looked in both directions before entering the second men's room I came across. I walked past urinals to a row of automatic sinks. Soap foam squirted into my hand with a two-part mechanical frog sound and I lathered up after adding a dash of water. I've never been diagnosed with any out-and-out disorders, but I do insist on a thorough hand washing.

After drying my hands—two depressions of the air dryer with my elbow—I turned to leave and everything seemed to break into frames. Standing at a urinal, upper torso and pixelated cephalic region turned toward me in a position he'd been holding for who knew how long, was the man. As I turned to flee the room, I caught his spectral image in the bathroom mirror, merging with the tile behind it before being swallowed by other hues. The phrase "through a glass darkly" (*dia spektrou*, referring to an imperfect image reflected in the bronze mirrors of the time) came to me unbidden.

I started to navigate the A-B-C-D-E pentagon (or was it an A-H octagon?) and put two terminals between myself and the figure. Yet another tantalizing explanation presented itself: I had been dosed with something, maybe in the coffee before my flight. I thought about the number of people alive who had witnessed the unexplainable, but could never reveal what they had seen for fear of ridicule.

I picked an empty gate, shielded my face with a newspaper, and poked a hole in it to monitor the flow of travelers. The terminal had taken on an otherworldly, liminal, temporary feel. Every passing traveler assumed I was on my way, or looked right through me, engrossed in where they would be in a few hours. My actions felt absurd, that is, until I saw the man in the suitcoat, his pace slowing before he passed, a human rendering of blurry video footage. I had the sensation that if he were to stop abruptly the blur might keep going before correcting itself.

Five minutes after the figure passed, I walked in the opposite direction and took a shuttle to the subway. Once out of the airport's immediate area, en route to sleep in a familiar place, the unreality of what I had seen began to dissipate. A series of sounds: PA announcements, doors opening and closing, footsteps, brake squeaks, distant traffic, an air brake hiss, clunking over tracks, a child yelling, music from other people's headphones, wind from a train on an adjacent track, clacks and thumps, a female voice, engine whine, brake release, a male voice, metal clang, distant tone, voices, water dripping, machine hum, distant scream, metal clink, tunnel wind, brake hiss, siren, clacking tracks, air release, bing-bong, hydraulic sound, light reverb, no sound.

2

The next morning, after a troubled sleep, I made plans to catch a matinee with my friend Liam. It was the firmly agoraphobic part of spring. The interval of occasional smiles from strangers had come to an end, and the city was no longer surprised, grateful for the onset of seasonal mood elevation. Sitting at my computer, still recovering from my blurry encounter in the airport, I experienced twin sensations: something had been taken from me, and something new and unfamiliar was now present. I manipulated the trackball on my mouse, watching the cursor move across the screen in ever-decreasing circles.

We agreed to meet at a subway stop, and I spotted Liam on the platform, head tilted down to focus on a book between his legs. He didn't notice me until I nudged his shoe. He closed his book and hid the cover, keeping it facedown on his knee. I don't think I need to point out what his name spells when read backward.

I told him about the conference on information destruction, but didn't mention the airport encounter. The day was too normal, the weather too pleasant, and I felt unable to articulate what I had seen, even to myself. Perhaps a suitable moment would present itself, or the memory would disintegrate, having been untold. My friend had related his share of questionable yarns, including his claim to have seen (from a distance, at night) multiple upright, simian, missing-link type creatures in the wilderness of the North Cascades. I resisted confiding in Liam, in part because I was afraid he would actually believe me.

I asked about the film we planned to see, which he said was obscure, foreign.

The subway car rattled as it neared the aboveground section of its path. Real light entered as we emerged, taking us over water. Liam and I observed structures in the water, statues. One looming pair consists of anthropoid metal forms rising 40 feet and appearing to grapple in the sightline of subway passengers and anyone on the nearby bridge. The figures are bent at the waist, leaning toward each other with limbs against shoulders as if exerting enormous forward pressure. There's another pair in Lisbon, I read somewhere. The world-renowned artist who designed them is dead now. Looking closer, I noticed a helicopter floating above the figures, its dangerous blades moving fast enough to present a blur. In four minutes we're back underground.

"But what's it about?" I asked.

It was hard to say. He'd seen a trailer that didn't reveal much. The director, an eccentric named Bevacqua, lived outside the city in a decrepit mansion on a forested estate, site of the tragic disappearance of a young couple and their three children, followed by the tragic reappearance of the couple and two-point-five children, a series of events that decreased the property's value in the eyes of the market and increased it in those of the director. The cult film was over twenty years in the making, and touted as a kind of love letter to a serial killer. Liam couldn't remember which one.

We left the subway before we had to and walked several blocks to the theater. All was covered in pollen, except for recently washed cars. Buildings most people no longer noticed rose around us. Liam was wearing a black t-shirt featuring his favorite filmmakers, twins, a shirt he wore at least twice each week.

We started talking about skyscrapers, *Wolkenkratzer*, cloudscratchers, the idea of supertall human structures as a triumph over nature, doing violence to the sky.

"I think the tallest building in the world is in Asia," he said.

"That's fine."

3

Outside the theater, a crowd at a sidewalk café had directed its attention to something on the roof of a parking garage across the street. I could only identify the bird as large. It may have been a hawk, an eagle, an Azure Gallinule, or a West Indian Whistling-Duck for all I knew; I'm no birder. An older woman pulled opera glasses from her purse, shouting "Oh my God!" and "Oh, Harold!" I'd seen all kinds of wildlife in major American cities: fox, wolf, bobcat, skunk, other things that would surprise you. The bird was likely watching for rats.

The film began with a close-up of a middle-aged man's face. He spoke in an accent that was difficult to identify: "It took a long time to conquer my worst childhood fear. But when I reached a certain age the fear started to make sense again." A series of long takes followed: a window-view of the street many stories below, a rooster pecking a snake to death, grainy footage I hoped was fake, an older woman in a red dress lying on a bed and repeating the phrase "clothes horse" until it lost all meaning, and an elaborate Powderpuff Chinese Crested beauty contest.

The majority of the film took place in spacious orange-lit concrete hallways. A voice spoke of a network of secret tunnels running under North America, the main artery of which overlapped with I-40 and ran a large portion of the 2,554 miles from Wilmington, North Carolina to Barstow, California. The route differed in that it bypassed Arkansas and Oklahoma completely, undercut Louisiana, and passed directly under Waco and Roswell. The network rejoined the interstate near Flagstaff, sharply deviating under Las Vegas and Death Valley. It also did a bit of a corkscrew out in the Nevada desert, somewhere around Groom Lake.

Two well-dressed men in a darkened room, identified by subtitles as "Site Facilitator" and simply "Harry," described the tunnels as a massive government project called "The Corridor" that had begun in the 1950's, shortly after the interstate highway system itself. It was a shadow interstate, in essence, that attempted to harness what are commonly known as Points of Power, hence its proximity to the aforementioned cities. According to Harry, not every U.S. President has known about the shadow system, only every other President, though he neglected to reveal the reason for alternating, who conveyed this knowledge, and whether the current President had been informed. The Corridor was smooth, rounded, and large enough to drive a bus through. The tunnel had been bored by a series of tunnel boring machines (TBMs) also known as "moles."

Footage of the orange hallway gave every impression of endlessness. The hallway scenes could have been filmed in the same, limited orange stretch and simply repeated, but I preferred to believe that the film contained a complete journey, captured in one take, then broken into pieces. The camera lingered on cryptic chalk-written signs:

This way to world's rarest fish

Valdeir Vieira was here

Mother always said: "There's a drawer in my desk I've never opened."

A species of pupfish known to dine on algae enriched by owl vomit

Following these messages, markings appeared in isolation on a wall:

O |

This was another symbol or a pair of them, as though the little letter on the figure's lapel had split into two. A little letter, if that's what it was, broken apart. But had the lowercase "a" divided mitotically into an "o" and an "I" (and was the latter an uppercase "I" or lowercase "l")? Looking closer, the first shape lacked even the slight ovality of the letter "o," more closely resembling the degree symbol, as in 99.5°, the temperature of my somewhat feverish body. The second shape may have been glyph rather than letter, one known as a vertical bar (found above the backslash on most keyboards) and many other names: sheffer stroke, conjunction negation, a.k.a. "not both" or "nand," obelisk, stick, glidus, and more.

There we sat in the second row of the nearly empty theater, no one between us and the light. I slouched in my seat, head tilted back to take in the whole screen. The cinema has always been a time to sleep, a religious service, a surgical procedure. At some point, an object or figure became apparent in the hallway's distance, growing slowly larger. Another sequence of images made it difficult to separate filler from whatever the opposite of filler is, à la alternating black and white bars of equal length that pop in and out depending on your focus. Filler: slow motion footage of a bird, bird's-eye footage of desert landscape overlaid with green grid and mobile targeting system, footage of actual torture. There were no title cards to indicate a beginning or an end, and clips appeared and repeated seemingly at random. For a time I was convinced the film was on a loop, that we had watched footage over and over, unawares. The final scene began with the approach of the distant figure—after ninety long seconds you could tell it was human. The camera paused for a moment before speeding up to pass the hallway figure: a man in a long black coat over a dark suit, collar, and tie. The face was, of course, a blur. Next to me, Liam mumbled. The camera advanced at an even quicker pace before the fade.

4

Outside in the declining sunlight, Liam and I debated the effects of matinees on healthy sleep patterns. When he mentioned the pixelation obscuring the figure's face, calling it disturbing, I said nothing. I wondered if the man in the film was the same as the man on the plane. Was one inspired by the other? In my state, it seemed possible that a living person could be based on a character in a film. I found myself scrutinizing the faces of every passing businessman in an overcoat.

A wave of dizziness washed over me. I had what could be referred to as "the spins." The film had dredged up parts of my airport experience. The most difficult image to shake was the figure's lack of facial features as I exited the bathroom: darker circular areas in an eye-eye-mouth configuration and obscured in the manner of heat shimmer, apparently staring. He had been standing there as if caught, or as if waiting for me.

Liam asked if I was OK, and I came back to myself, eyes closed and fingertips at each temple. I felt fine, I told him.

I asked myself again what exactly I had seen, and if I had really seen it. Of course I had seen it, but had others? The filmic "effect," as Liam had called it, was easy enough to explain: a film editor had added the blur after the fact. Or had they? Was the figure actually in possession of a formless, shifting cranio-facial region, and did the camera merely document this with accuracy? Doubtful. Did the figure possess some cutting-edge projection technology, capable of presenting a certain face to 99.9999% of observers, a technology that had failed, in my case? Was I a member of the .0001%? If only. Could any of this be independently verified? What was the man's condition? And again: did the man from the airport actually have a role in the film we'd just seen?

By this time, Liam wanted to talk, to drink, wanted a gram of this or 100 milligrams of that—I didn't object. I felt like a character in a film myself, except one who had no script, no acting ability, no idea what the movie was about, and in fact no idea he was in a film at all. It was *cinéma-vérité-vérité*. We walked to a place that was mobbed, and left it for a place whose logo suggested style to women and sex to men.

After we ordered, Liam asked around for our mutual friend who could usually be found near the bar area. Given today's events, I decided to go along with his plan. I asked what else he knew about the director.

"His last name is Bevacqua. His nationality is disputed," he said.

"Disputed?"

"Or unclear. No one knows where he's actually from. He claims to have been born in France, but his accent sounds fake."

"What do you know about the title?" I asked.

"*Pupfish*? They're a kind of desert fish—found in the southwest. In interviews he suggests it's a multi-lingual pun."

I asked him how he knew all this, and he mentioned a series of websites. One old message board in particular was called "Charles Manson's Desert Hole."

"There goes my workday tomorrow," I said. My phone vibrated.

A text message:

xxx-xxx-xxxx: I can see you.

I knew the number well, though I had deleted the owner's name from my phone at least a year before. Though we were back on good terms, it would take too long for me to enter Bobbi Jo Ashworth-Portendorfer's full name again. I scanned the bar, saw her with friends, and waved. There had been some good times.

One of my therapists took Bobbi Jo Ashworth-Portendorfer's name and ran with it in the manner of some single-mindedly manic sports analogy, using it to first initiate a line of questioning, and then to put forward assertions of increasing bluntness that an unconscious part of my attraction to Bobbi Jo Ashworth-Portendorfer was a result of her traditionally male Christian name, one she furthermore shared with my father, and that yet another one of many unconscious parts of my attraction to Bobbi Jo Ashworth-Portendorfer, given my association of her with my father, was my Oedipal desire to kill her/kill my father, which in this case "kill" meant penetrate and have intercourse with, sex as coupled with violence not being the freshest concept ever devised, granted. Bobbi Jo Ashworth-Portendorfer looked nothing like Robert Joseph, may he rest in peace.

She looked happy, though I may have attributed happiness to others after Liam gave me a pink pill and a yellow one, round and oblong respectively, and after I started on my second drink. The way things usually went with Bobbi and me was akin to my conception of history, that is to say: cyclical.

Bobbi was standing with friends (two female, one male) around a too-small table crowded with empty glasses: beer, rocks, martini, tumbler. Her friends had names like Joy, Leo, and Avery, and seemed to frown with a collective eyebrow. They had been discussing a most serious matter. Bobbi introduced everyone. Joy maintained a washed out smile, Avery was ebullient, and Leo gave the slightest of nods. He seemed disappointed that we'd shown up, as if agitated he was no longer the only emitter of certain smells. If there had been televisions in the bar, they would have shown footage of angry crowds rioting in the aftermath of Xianjiang bomb blasts. Possible phrasings would have included "How the demonstrations became violent is unclear" and "Multiple simultaneous bomb detonations in China's Xinjiang province, specifically in Ürümqi, the capital of the XUAR (Xinjiang Uyghur Autonomous Region), were followed by protests which led to looting, fighting, and vandalism in the streets" and "It has come to light that the Xinjiang Guanghui Flying Tigers professional basketball team of the Chinese Basketball association had been killed in the blast." Then commentary.

"… a projected world power since, like, forever."

"Shanghai? Shenzen?"

"So ancient, so rich."

"…grander scales, new methods and technologies, wider media dissemination."

"So-called 'black prisons.' Privately run. Soundproofed hotel rooms you can't leave as long as someone pays to keep you there."

"…by definition a modern phenomenon."

"Mao?"

"Kissinger."

"The total land area of the U.S. is roughly 3,700,000 square miles."

"Rome and The British Empire are not models. Gigi Hadid, however…"

"A tragedy, sure. But a capital-T tragedy?"

5

I was late to work the next day, commuting as I was from Bobbi's apartment. My employer, Shred Authority Neighborhood Storage (SANS), had an office with an attached warehouse outside the city, practically in a suburb, on a side street next to an organic grocery. Document storage and shredding is more exciting than it sounds. We did secure paper storage and electronic record storage, document scanning, microfilm and microfiche conversion, radio frequency tracking, we did shredding. Boy did we do shredding. Onsite and off. With witnesses if you wanted.

I unlocked, turned on the lights, the computer, the scanner, placed shredders in standby mode, looked at the list of appointments. The owner, a man named Edgar whose last name was on the brink of extinction, was not in. I sat in the full-body shiatsu massage chair he had recently purchased, and regarded a painting of a lotus flower. I could hear muffled street noise—honking cars and the sound of a helicopter. Maybe it was a traffic helicopter, or one in pursuit of a fugitive. When I heard knocks from the street entrance, I turned off the chair, went to the door, and opened it for a balding woman in a short-sleeve dress shirt, abbreviated tie, and spectacles. She resembled a substitute teacher, and was carrying a document box with handles that she placed on the counter.

The woman asked how did I do. I wondered what her life was like, whether she was a CIA subcontractor. That would have been unlikely, since all major government agencies have sophisticated shredding equipment themselves.

She inquired about our shredding charges and I explained the various security levels (1-6) and our pricing plans. We also offered pulping, pulverizing, and chemical decomposition, though these are rarely requested. The woman said she wanted something between your conventional office shredder and your highest security shredder, which can turn an 8 1/2" x 11" sheet into over 15,000 particles. I led her to our 650-Sheet Cross-Cut Shredder/Baler Combo. It's gorgeous.

She handed over the box and I removed a layer of papers from the neat stack inside, measuring 500 sheets by touch. I checked for paperclips and other metal items; the blades can handle credit cards but nothing much sturdier. I woke the shredder and inserted the ream into its 20" throat. Her demeanor edged toward nervous with her documents exposed. Working this job early on, I used to feign disinterest for the clients' benefit while eyeballing everything I could, though the need to do so waned quickly. I never saw a single intriguing piece of paper enter a shredder in all my time at SANS. What we have in storage, however, is a different story.

I didn't really care what people wanted gone, any more than I cared about their grooming habits. Usually it was medical information, legal documents, or materials related to royalties that had to be destroyed in view of witnesses, who would sign to this effect. My interest was no longer piqued when individuals showed up in trench coats, suit coats, gun coats, weather-inappropriate rain coats, or bathrobes, carrying briefcases filled with photographs and negatives they wanted destroyed beyond all hope of reconstruction. I had no desire to pry when the occasional celebrity, washed-up or otherwise, came around. I was a professional.

The shredder was more expensive than your average automobile, with a shred speed of 42 feet per minute. I continued loading its throat. The woman's formerly heavy document box diminished. Her comportment reminded me of a museum security guard worried a visitor is about to get too close. I myself was wary of the machine—that had never waned. The vast majority of shredder injuries happen to children in the home. What did people mean when they said "images come unbidden?" They came to me all the time, usually images of an arm entering the throat of our largest industrial shredder.

I gave the woman her empty box, her load lightened by about 2,500 sheets. She paid with cash and we wished one another a pleasant remainder of the day.

With no customers in sight, I was able to indulge my curiosity about Bevacqua, and by extension the blurry character from the airport. I opened a secure browser on my office computer and looked up directors named Bevacqua. Very little information was available. I found poorly written and visually jarring fan pages, online encyclopedia entries that regurgitated the same content into each other's mouths. Searching for "Charles Manson's Desert Hole" turned up numerous pages documenting Manson's belief that he had found the entrance to a Bottomless Pit in the desert, which was actually an entrance to a cave system filled with salt water and heated by a geothermal spring. A kind of pupfish lives there and only there: *Cyprinodon diabolis.* I could find no website of the same name, though searching for "Bevacqua and Manson hole" led to a discussion forum for obscure and experimental films. One message thread on the site:

FilmNut808: where can I find this movie? i've been looking for years

jollyharry: send me an email and i'll put you in touch with the director

VOIDENTERER420: THIS MOVIE ISN'T EVEN REAL LOL

PersonaLover: Do not pursue this. I happen to know this film is real, and it should be banned. Watching it has sent me into a spiral I can't escape.

The website made it seem that the film I had viewed was only part of a much longer project, which made sense when I considered its disjointed nature and short run time. Everything I learned was etched into my brain. I already slept poorly, but the idea of a website named after a movie named after a desert hole, real or imagined, was somehow terrifying. I felt a connection to the anonymous commenters on the site, especially the one who felt trapped in a spiral by the *Pupfish* film. Not only did I feel a connection, but I had the sense I might be them in another life.

6

After work I went to a secret room in the public library that was filling up with my trash. The room was never really secret, but no one else seemed to show up. One reached it via a basement hallway, by opening a door behind a door. The minor trashcan housed empty paper coffee cups, soda cans, bags from pastry shops with crumpled cookie sheets inside, tissues laden with my genetic material. The residue of sugar in the cans occasionally attracted ants—I managed to tidy up once per quarter.

The room contained a chair, tiny desk, and aforementioned trashcan. I felt a kinship with these objects. Sometimes I even reminded myself of furniture, like a skeletal wingback chair in a crocodile hornback cut. As a small child, I used to think I was a footstool, and that other pieces of furniture were my friends and relatives. Sitting in a large chair was like sitting on the lap of a huggable grandparent who could engulf you. Chairs stacked in the corner of the school gym were obscene in the way they hinted at a circus-like people pyramid. Chairs have arms, legs, backs, and seats (bums). My mother was a sometimes elegant 1960s end table with a glass top. My father became a coffee table, for obvious reasons.

I had the hots for one of the sofas, liver-colored or maybe even a raw umber. Basically, it was brown; curvy and enormous, with decadent pillows and tailored cushions to die for. It was corduroy, and made me misapprehend the word "loveseat" for years. The couch and I had relations.

We'd rendezvous late at night, or when my parents left us home alone, which didn't happen until my sisters were a little older. They were puzzled, repulsed, amused, and—at bottom—just a little bit jealous. Maggie was a credenza, Sandra some kind of shoe-tree or coat-rack (she was quite tall).

The library had fewer distractions, though information on Bevacqua remained difficult to find. It emerged that his first name was Lucian, though if Lucian Bevacqua didn't sound like a made up name I don't know what did. Internet searches yielded a company called Pupfish Productions, and a set designer for *The Young and the Restless* named Steven Bevacqua, but not much else. Reliable information was scanty, but I came across a rumor site with extensive archives. Reading the comment threads, I felt the need to look over my shoulder. Some seemed melodramatic at best, others rather unsettling.

Stop searching while you still can.

By coming here you've put yourself in danger.

I'd like to learn more about you.

Still others seemed fabricated, and once the possibility occurred to me, I was unable to read conversations on the site without thinking both sides had been written by the same person. Or maybe that *all* comments on the site had the same author. One thread caught my eye, titled:

Tell me about this image and I'll tell you more

The thread, which had no responses, featured an image of the faceless man resembling a still from the *Pupfish* film: the figure in profile against a concrete wall in orange light, head turned toward the viewer, though with all detail blurred away. As usual, a surveillance video face. Looking at the image, I had the sensation of being watched, but also of watching myself: typing, searching, chasing leads in pursuit of—what?

Was it a film still or separate footage? And what was the source of the distortion? I clicked on the username of the poster, clicked "send message," and felt myself grow dizzy. I became convinced that someone knew I was looking at the image, and that I had irrevocably established a link, via this person, to something else, something large.

The spins hit me again, full-on. I couldn't be sure how long I had closed my eyes. I sent a message, and was prompted to create a username:

SANSman: Pupfish?

I hit refresh and saw a red (1) indicating a new message.

Conduit187: the film you saw was only a preview

SANSman: how do i see more?

Conduit187: by following my instructions to the letter

The cursor became uncooperative, turned into the rainbow Spinning Beach Ball of Death. I hit "refresh" again, and a notification appeared: "The post you are looking for has been deleted by the user." Clicking on Conduit187 generated "user does not exist." A search yielded no results, either for the user or the image post. I should have saved the photo the instant it appeared— now the only record I had was my memory.

7

I first met Blanche at another screening of *Pupfish*, held at a local film club, which I discovered by scouring the Internet for all information related to Lucian Bevacqua, the *Pupfish* film, and men with pixelated faces. This activity now occupied nearly all my waking hours, including those on the clock at SANS. When I did manage to sleep, my dreams were peopled with blurred visages on flights, in corridors, in stairwells, in corners, hovering next to my bed. I woke up sweating, dry-mouthed, and frequently dizzy. The screening of *Pupfish* came out of the blue, as did a chance meeting and conversation with Blanche. She ended up inviting me to come along with the crowd to a nearby party, post-screening. She was wearing a t-shirt that said "I Want to Want to Believe." One of many other features that drew me to her was a text tattoo on her inner forearm:

This, more than the last symbol, was truly legible as an actual letter. To an observer facing Blanche, the tattoo depicted the letter "i," its tittle or diacritic dot a large bubble. From Blanche's perspective, the tattoo could be read as an exclamation point. She claimed, over the course of the night, that it was variously: a mechanically separated lollipop, the sun above the tree of life, a depiction of the path from the material to the spirit realm, and half a fish bladder facing penetration. The night we met played over in my mind, on a loop, for quite some time.

8

Blanche's apartment was lined with wall-to-wall bookshelves, seemingly organized by theme. I asked what her absent roommate thought of the reading material.

"We've known each other long enough," she said.

"She doesn't wonder about you?"

Blanche laughed. "It's just research."

I read some titles out loud, like *Women Serial Killers of the 20th Century, Killer Clown,* and *Natural Born Celebrities: Serial Killers in American Culture.* Row upon row that would have given a sober visitor pause.

"What do you do besides attend weird film screenings?" she asked. She stood up and went to the door, shooting the deadbolt. She turned on a record player, and I watched it spin in endless loops. The moving text was impossible to read, but Blanche told me it was Glenn Gould performing Brahms.

I told her I worked at a document storage and shredding facility, that I was doing research of my own, that I fantasized about picking up other people's photos from the drug store.

"No one knows about *Pupfish*," she said. "Or regular people don't."

"I guess I appreciate oddities."

"What else?"

"Obscure films in old formats."

"Like from garage sales? Estate sales?"

"Sure. Even old home videos can be interesting."

She asked me if I liked to travel, if I was a frequent flier, looking at me in a strange way, smiling. Did she know something? She asked me if I wanted another beer. I thanked her and scanned titles after she left the room.

Killer Apps: Murder in the Digital Age

Men Who Love Women Who Love Men Who Kill

Mass Murder in the United States

The Serial Killer Whisperer

Killing It: Serial Killers and Success in the Workplace

She came back with a beer and we sat at opposite ends of a long couch. People are intrigued when they catch themselves doing something against their nature, or reacting in an atypical way, which in my case was not wanting to move closer to Blanche on the couch. I found myself in some heretofore concealed pocket of unknowing.

"What's the appeal?" I asked, gesturing to the shelves.

She said something about a fixation on power, on glamour, the way reading such disturbing material managed to merge fascination and nausea in an inexplicable way.

"You act like I admitted to collecting and polishing Nazi memorabilia."

"Well," I said.

Something struck me about serial killers, particularly the "serial" part. Unless the killer was stopped, each victim served as a link in an ever-extending chain, part of a process that repeated without end. Early theories, in fact, referred to serial killers as "repeat killers."

The record stopped, and Blanche rose to restart the process. She asked me again if I liked flying. She mentioned she had friends she'd like me to meet. Film buffs, collectors, other people. She said she saw me at the film screening.

"I know, I was there."

"No," she said. "I mean the other one. The one before."

9

I didn't remember nodding off, or how a blanket had found me, or the last topic of conversation before sleep. I assumed Blanche was on her way to work. A note urged me to keep in touch, asked me to lock the front door by pushing the doorknob's button on my way out. I scribbled a reply and hurried to the street.

After walking for a time, illogically pleased to have escaped Blanche's building without encountering anyone, a question occurred to me: Had I locked her front door? The ground floor exit had already locked behind me, which was both a comfort and an obstacle to any potential return. I found myself thinking of various objects with a locked exterior and some open door inside them, all day long. Desks with hidden drawers. A hidden panel inside a locked drawer inside a closed rolltop desk. The concept was somehow unnerving.

My boss had left me a queue of six bundles for shredding. I turned on the lights and carried the first bundle to a position near the shredders, which I activated. While the shredders warmed up, I visited a video-sharing website. Searches that yielded nothing of much relevance included:

man with blurry face
man in long hallway
America's longest corridor
transcontinental passageways
man in orange conduit

I searched for "Conduit187" (to see if the user had

commented on other websites) to no avail, and checked the rumor site where I first learned about the film's mysterious director. On the homepage I found a tab that either I had overlooked, or wasn't previously visible. The tab said "TRADE," and took me to a page where users posted links, uploaded, and discussed the films of Lucian Bevacqua. I was, as they say, hooked. Bevacqua had dozens, if not hundreds, of films to his credit. Like Kenneth Anger, he worked almost exclusively in the medium of short films. One of the most popular threads on the forum, closed after hundreds of comments, was titled "The turn: LB's post-2001 involvement with surveillance footage collage." In addition to a raging debate, the post featured numerous examples of this era of Bevacqua's art, including a film that purported to depict one young woman's epic crosstown shopping spree, cobbled together from street CCTV footage and security camera footage from each store she visited.

I received a new message, and noted the address of the new forum for further study. The message's subject line read "DEAD DROP." Unease caused me to search for the term itself, which turned out to be a method of exchanging items without the simultaneous presence of both parties. I got the spins something awful.

A loose brick in a wall, a cut-out book, a hole in a tree

The user calling him- or herself Conduit187 wanted to exchange information as a means of building trust, as prelude to a discussion concerning a certain "obscured individual of mutual relation."

The message said, if I agreed, I was to designate a time and place for the drop. To begin with, all he or she wanted from me at the drop point was the date, time, and duration of my encounter with "our mutual friend of blurred visage." I specified 2:00pm at the base of a statue by a courtyard fountain, near the downtown library, and was informed to expect reciprocation at the same spot within 24 hours.

I wrote on a small piece of paper before folding it in half twice:

20th of April: 8:46am, 9:03am, 10:19am, 10:31am

I closed Shred Authority early and took the subway into the city. The station map brought to mind the film's oddball musings about the shadow highway system. I found myself thinking about meridians, pathways in the body, energy flows. At least twelve U.S. states are home to towns called Meridian, some more than one. Eisenhower too, father of the Interstate, died of congestive heart failure—a failure of circulation within his own system.

The symbols I had encountered of late, their odd illegibility, raised the possibility of language impairment. Aphasia, possibly brought on by head trauma. Or was I thinking of an entirely different condition? I scrutinized the face of every person on the subway, then on the street—none were distorted. Did I have a kind of selective blindness, was the face of just one man affected by a neurological disorder of mine? Propo-something? Proso-something? One term related to language, one to faces.

I studied the face of a man in a suit jacket over an open-collared white dress shirt, the face of a woman in a grey velour tracksuit, the faces of elderly tourists waiting for the crossing signal. I speculated about their inner lives.

The courtyard fountains were dry this time. I placed the folded piece of paper in the hollow at the base of a statue. It was a pretty good statue: female, clothed, bronze, cupping a bowl to her lips, a bowl out of which water would stream when the pump came on. I squatted to nudge my communiqué further in, and noticed another scrap, highlighter yellow, that I pinched with two fingers. I stood, and headed for the library, thinking I should have circled the area before making the drop. I observed a façade containing a window containing a face, before a curtain closed in front of it.

I entered the library, started to look like I belonged there, and removed the yellow piece of paper from my pocket.

Your cooperation is valuable and much appreciated. The person we discussed is possibly aware of your movements. Discontinue use of previous drop point.

I roamed the modern wing—made of mostly glass— until I found a restroom. Someone was in the stall next to mine, doing something that made a lot of noise, bumping against the partition, and scuffing the floor with his feet. Maybe he was changing his clothes, jerking off, doing intravenous drugs, or maybe there was more than one person over there. The floor looked like marble or imitation marble, heavily waxed, and looking down, the level of detail available in my reflection disturbed me.

The need to relieve myself was second to my desire to dispose of the message I had found. I dangled the paper over the bowl, keeping a safe distance from its invisible aura, and watched it see-saw down, coming to rest on the bowl's inner rim. This was most disappointing. Nevertheless, by some feat of concentration, and without using my hands, I was able to knock the scrap of paper from roughly the 7 o'clock position into the bowl.

I may have made a sound when an unfamiliar foot entered the space of my stall, then withdrew in an awkward, lazy arc. The partition rattled as something slammed into the other side. I heard the sound of fabric sliding down the plastic barrier, and a head appeared in my stall. Fumbling with the lock behind me, I performed some lurching combination of tripping over and kicking the human head below. His mouth was open and he didn't look conscious.

No one was in the hallway when I left the bathroom, though I would've ploughed through any bodies regardless. I had likely pissed myself at least a little, but there was also major relief: the man in the stall was a normal street person. I was able to make out all his facial features.

After making my way upstairs, through quiet hallways into another wing, I realized I had failed to flush. Had been prevented from flushing. Was the homeless man homeless, or was he someone else, someone in the employ, or briefly under the control, of those who wanted access to the paper? I should have kept it, without a doubt, if only to examine the handwriting. Perhaps the note had contained an unseen instruction, hidden in the text or applied with a drop of liquid the smell of which would serve as a kind of nerve agent, instructing the receiver to destroy the message. It wasn't impossible. I resolved to investigate when I could be sure my visitor had moved on.

The nearby seating area only had two patrons: a sweaty man flipping through a large textbook faster than typical reading might require, and a woman sitting across from him, erratically shouting a series of instructions, criticisms, questions, and abuse. I stood and watched until I noticed a row of dictionaries in a shielded aisle, and moved to observe them through the stacks. I found the biggest dictionary I could and began flipping through the P's.

polyptych n. a painting, especially an altarpiece, consisting of more than three leaves or panels joined by hinges or folds.

polytunnel n. an elongated polythene-covered frame under which plants are grown outdoors.

polyuria n. production of abnormally large volumes of dilute urine.

prosopagnosia n. an inability to recognize the faces of familiar people, typically as a result of damage to the brain.

I shifted to the B's, in what seemed a logical move (inversion of the P).

brothel creepers pl. n. informal soft-soled suede shoes.

Brocken specter n. a magnified shadow of an observer, typically surrounded by rainbow-like bands, thrown on to a bank of cloud in high mountain areas when the sun is low.

Broca's area n. Anatomy a region of the brain concerned with the production of speech, located in the cortex of the dominant frontal lobe.

branks pl. n. historical an instrument of punishment for a scolding woman, consisting of an iron framework for the head and a sharp metal gag for restraining the tongue. [cf German Pranger a pillory or bit for a horse]

boggart (Scottish and N. English) / bogeyman / bogey n. an evil or mischievous spirit bilocation n. the supposed phenomenon of being in two places simultaneously.

bibliomancy n. the practice of foretelling the future by interpreting a randomly chosen passage from a book, especially the Bible.

Before leaving, I decided to check the library's audio holdings. They had a great deal of Glenn Gould, so much that I hoped I would find the record Blanche had played in her apartment. After nearly giving up, I found a single copy of the album in question: a recording of Glenn Gould performing Brahms. According to the man himself, "It's the sexiest interpretation of Brahms's Intermezzi you've ever heard—and I really think it is perhaps the best piano playing I have done. You know what an incurable romantic I am anyway." I was attracted to the idea of a short piece—an *intermezzo*—meant to connect larger works, and the fact that here were ten pieces of connecting tissue all by themselves. Ten fragments that made a larger fragment. I replayed my memory of the night I met Blanche, editing it to change the outcome.

On the way out, I performed recon at the site of my bathroom trauma. When no one was within view of the door, I went inside, bending down to check each stall. I stood in the doorway of the one I'd used earlier, reluctant to commit myself to full entry. I peered into the bowl until curiosity brought me forward. The liquid there looked identical to what I could recall—a pale lemon chiffon— but there was no visible paper.

I reasoned that the possibilities were five, minimum. The paper may have dissolved. Or someone had flushed the toilet, and the same person (or one following) had replaced my urine with their own. Or the toilet had been urinated into, flushed, and urinated into again so as to appear unchanged. Or the paper had floated into an area of the bowl hidden from view. Or, perhaps, someone had retrieved the paper and left my urine.

10

Some days later, I found myself back at Blanche's apartment, on the verge of bringing up recent puzzling events. As with Liam, something held me back. It wasn't that I didn't trust Blanche, though we barely knew one another, but I wasn't ready to start a conversation that could end with so many unreal assertions. I didn't want to appear unhinged, though again, as with Liam, my greater fear may have been that Blanche would actually believe me, considering her own eccentricities.

An *intermezzo* filled the air. Watching the record slowly rotate, I had the thought that I was *in between* myself. Filler. Like an extra in a film, or one of many interchangeable parts that could be shuffled about at will. Watching the record's circular path, I couldn't help but think of helicopter blades, a film projector. Blanche spoke, as if reading my mind:

"Glenn Gould thought of himself as akin to a film director, you know," she said.

"How's that?" I asked.

"He wasn't averse to editing. To cobbling together a recording, of Bach, say, out of multiple takes."

She said it's something we take for granted, but was visionary at the time. Gould invited sound professionals to try and find the splices, which they usually couldn't.

"The tape lies," she said. "And gets away with it."

A white cat that I never saw or heard on my previous visit jumped onto the coffee table, watched the spinning record under its case. I projected a complex inner life onto her.

It's funny, the longer I sat on Blanche's couch thinking about my lack of agency, the more I wanted to make love. I wasn't certain that Blanche knew this, but I suspected she had some idea. When she said she wanted to take me somewhere, I nursed the desperate hope that she meant to take me to bed, while I knew without a doubt that our destination would have something to do with the faceless man I had seen on the flight.

11

Blanche took me to where she worked, a hulking glass structure inside an isolated industrial park. Entering, we passed towering plants and rusted metal statues with spindly limbs that looked like they wanted to disappear. She signed us in with security, swiped her ID at a bank of elevators, swiped again inside an elevator, and chose a floor in the 20s. She had changed her wacky clothes to dark jeans and a dress shirt before driving us to the central offices of so-called Vector Industries. I felt residual lust and fantasized about an elevator malfunction. To distract myself, I asked Blanche what they did at Vector Industries, and she said something about data storage. I considered the word "vector" for a while.

We got off at a floor in the 20s and proceeded down gray, carpeted hallways past a series of empty cubicles. Blanche walked quickly, ID lanyard swinging in circular arcs in her hand. The next elevator required the entry of a key code in addition to an ID swipe before opening. We had taken sufficient turns for me to have completely forgotten the way.

The second elevator was large enough to make me wonder if its purpose was to carry freight. An SUV could have fit inside without difficulty, though of course it couldn't have been driven down the hallway. The doors continued to retract behind the walls, and I imagined even larger portals on other levels. I followed Blanche as she entered, swiped yet again, and pressed the button marked "-3." The floors below this level were not listed as numbers, but rather a series of Xs.

The elevator seemed to have slowed a great deal once below the lobby. I stared at the series of X's, which seemed etched into the elevator metal. The X's seemed to become more deeply etched the longer I looked. I felt a wave of dizziness. I had the spins again, though the movement of the elevator suggested nothing of that kind of motion. I leaned on the wall, waiting for the sensation to pass or for Blanche to ask about my wellbeing. We made it to an unnumbered level, site of a square room, gray light, and a receptionist in a sensible gray skirt, whatever that meant.

The receptionist signed us in, and when I looked again and she was wearing white: what looked like an old fashioned nurse's uniform dress. The light in the room changed, as though a dimmer switch had been almost imperceptibly turned, subtle enough to leave doubt as to whether the power had flickered.

The receptionist stood up, smiling. She was now wearing a doctor's coat and a stethoscope around her neck. "Right this way," she said. She seemed able to play the part of nearly any role you could throw at her. I had the distinct impression that I was both watching a film and attempting to find my legs within one.

Blanche's expression was enigmatic enough to mean nearly anything. I couldn't discern whether she was reacting to, or even aware, of the receptionist's appearance, whose clothing shifts resembled continuity errors in a film.

The receptionist, now wearing gray slacks, approached a metal door at the back wall, glancing over her shoulder and winking as we followed. Or did she actually wink? Doubtful. She keyed the keypad, slid her badge, and let Blanche and I inside another hallway with gray carpeting. Blanche turned to me when the door closed behind us. A click followed the sound of the door closing by a few seconds.

"[unintelligible]," she said.

The hallway featured eight gray doors with metal handles, four on each wall, before turning at a right angle. I had the urge to ask Blanche what she knew about the man whose face was blurred, but felt it would be rash. What little power I had stemmed from what I had seen on the plane, what I knew about Bevacqua's film, and what I chose to reveal. I asked Blanche what her title was and she said she recorded visitor responses to video. Her response included the words "specialist," "supervisor," or possibly "analyst." The hallway carpet made me think of the airport, and I pictured the transportation links from there to this building: air, rail, automobile, helicopter. Vehicles coming and going, replaced and refueled on a loop, bodies moving in a similarly circular pattern.

"Where are your coworkers?"

"All around," she said, leaning against the wall.

"I don't see any," I said. "What kind of video do you analyze?"

She asked if I wanted to view some myself, and I said I did. According to her, each of the eight visible doors, in addition to others, led to rooms containing video footage. She wouldn't reveal how they were organized, if at all. I felt surrounded by circles—camera lenses and clocks—and fought off a wave of dizziness. Even if you don't literally clock in, you're on the clock, subject to the circular movement of three hands. I fantasized about hitting the "refresh" button on my brain.

I ruled out the initial doors on my left and right as "too soon." Ditto the second pair of doors. Both doors #3 were incredibly tempting, though tempting enough to be too predictable. Moving towards door #4 on the right, I hesitated. This door happened to be the last before the bend in the hallway. I settled on door #2 on my right, possibly too "even" a combination of second door and recto, possibly a serious mistake.

I pushed open the door, and entered a dark room lit by blue light issuing from a peephole-sized hole. The door closed behind me, followed by a click. Was Blanche watching me now, was anyone else? I moved to the wall. Viewed from the side, the peephole functioned as a projector in the small room, *camera obscura*. Dust particles—I hesitate to call them motes—were on the move. I put my eye to the peephole.

I had trouble believing that the image I saw was on a screen. The quality was such that one could be forgiven for thinking the back wall of this dark room abutted a spacious bathroom with dark tile, a recessed niche for towels, and a man absorbed in the screen of his phone. I stood, removing my eye from the hole, instinctively sure that if I could see the man, he could see me. I looked again and was treated to a neck-to-waist view of a man, phone in hand. As I crouched and observed, my field of view shifted, moving closer to the phone and tilting slightly. The phone was nothing special, cutting edge, black, rectangular, a screen that you touch.

The man's phone loomed closer, or rather its screen became the only thing I could see. I was observing a man in a bathroom somewhere watching porn on a very large phone indeed. Had I put my eye to the peephole at that moment, I would've had no clue that the video was being played on a phone, no idea about the layers involved.

My point of entry, surveillance footage of a man standing in a bathroom, had now been effaced. The phone he still presumably held happened to display video of a man standing in a bathroom, though this video quickly became far more engaging. This latter bathroom was large, public, of single-occupancy design, with hand-dryer, sink, and a handrail next to the toilet. I was unsure whether this was a set, actually. This man stood with his back to the camera, his face visible in the mirror over the sink. His expression was common to pornographic productions of even high quality: a wide-eyed attempt at conveying emotion, resulting in a mixture of puzzlement, profundity, and self-aware comedy.

The actor sighed and splashed water in his face, running his hands slowly down. He was wearing a dress shirt, and a tie he loosened theatrically. The door creaked in a manner at odds with the sound of nearly any public restroom door, followed by the sound, delayed, of a door slamming shut. A woman, endowed in ways that complemented those of the man, entered the frame wearing a skirt and high heels. The image of heels coming in contact with the tile was out of sync with the sound of heel clicks by a full second, creating a strange tension.

The man said the equivalent of "What on earth are you doing here?" as his earlier expression somehow intensified. "I think you know," she said, and began attacking his shirt buttons. As her own blouse came off, the image started to shake rhythmically, disrupting the illusion of unity in this new situation. The man's shirt was on the floor, his pants around his ankles, the woman was naked save for heels, and bent over in the position of a diver, with both hands on the sink. The mirror provided an additional frontal viewing angle. Movement of the phone made screen obvious qua screen again, and my hand moved to my crotch in a half-hearted way. I wondered if Blanche was watching me, and doing the same. I wondered if someone was watching her, and doing the same.

I tried the door to the hallway, which remained locked. After banging on it with my fist, I started walking back toward the peephole when I heard the click of the lock mechanism. I wandered out into the hallway and found Blanche more or less where she had been before. Her expression, once again, was difficult to gauge.

"You picked a good one," she said. There was a hint of a smile there—maybe she was pregnant.

I asked her if the feed was live, and she said all of them were, though they also had playback capability.

"So where is that guy?"

"He's local," she said.

The funny thing about pornography is the actors often know that the assets on view aren't their acting chops. There's an element of willfully bad acting that can add a certain charge to the whole enterprise. Or perhaps not even bad acting, but acting that draws attention to itself as such. They know they're acting, you know they're acting, and they know you know, etc. It's akin to writing a sentence while remaining aware of the sentence's artifice.

What I had just viewed was live footage from a private residence, footage a client wanted monitored for some reason. Vector's clients varied from surveillance enthusiasts, to suspicious spouses, to scientists seeking data on human behavior, to numerous law enforcement agencies. As a private contractor, Vector was able to access nearly any video footage in the city. Home security systems. CCTVs on streetlamps. The cameras at 7-Eleven. Webcams. Many of the feeds, such as convenience stores and the like, were provided voluntarily in the event that specific footage would need to be accessed. The rest were open access, one way or another.

Blanche led me to a room filled with computers and thin blue carpet over concrete. Two large screens formed a V dominating one corner—the rest was divided into cubicles featuring a monitor on each desk. She turned on the largest screen, a projector, and the company's logo appeared in a field of black, morphed into a blue and white diamond-patterned expanse. She brought up a long list of names, nearly all male.

"This is our freelance pool, though some of them don't know it yet," she said. "Each one of these men—a few women here and there—specialize in spying on other people's computers. Usually for laughs, occasionally for voyeurism, at least initially."

She opened the file of one "Grayson Blanco," bringing up his photo, date of birth (he was in his mid-forties), social security number, address, place of birth, phone number, and IP address. She said he was one of many who used something called a Remote Administration Tool (RAT) to spy on victims. RATters, as they were called, exploited vulnerabilities in computer systems, or simply tricked users, in order to install software that let them control the webcam. Users victimized in this way were referred to as "slaves," the most desirable of which were attractive young women, the most desirable of which walked around their apartments naked, in a towel, or scantily clad, chatted frequently while naked, and so on.

Blanche zoomed out to "show all." The screen populated with video feeds: dozens of faces bathed in blue-white light, empty bedrooms, empty offices, empty living rooms, empty chairs, empty couches, views from open laptops and desktops. From this field of faces and vacant rooms, she selected Grayson Blanco, who appeared to be eating something while typing. From Blanco, she selected a dropdown menu that brought up another field of faces. These were computers Blanco controlled, nine in number. The content of the various feeds was as follows:

Screen #1: A young woman, brunette, wearing a hooded sweatshirt, eyes moving in a fashion that suggested reading text on screen. Background over her shoulder appeared to be a college dorm room.

Screen #2: Inactive, black screen.

Screen #3: A young woman, also brunette, wearing glasses and headphones. Lips moving, and likely engaged in video chat.

Screen #4: Inactive, black screen.

Screen #5: Empty leather desk chair in a room painted red.

Screen #6: Dark room, featuring bed with one or two unidentifiable lumps.

Screen #7: A young woman, blonde, in robe and wearing a towel on her head.

Screen #8: Living room, dimly lit, with couch and book shelf (titles not legible).

Screen #9: Inactive, black screen.

"You probably know I didn't bring you here for kicks," Blanche said. She enlarged the screen with the red room and empty chair. Looking closer I noticed the corner of a calendar, though the month was off-screen. As I considered the women who didn't know they were being surveilled, I had the realization that I was living my life, had been living my life for some time, under the growing impression that everything I did was recorded. Growing up, everyone seemed to have this suspicion. Adults, children, actors in films and on television, the media, the jokes, the paranoid hangover of an age of analog wiretapping. The only difference now was the certainty and depth of the scrutiny.

"I'm having a great time," I said.

"The room we're seeing belongs to a former employee of this company, a man you saw on your flight a few days ago."

"What's his name?" I asked.

She said the name they had on file was false, that almost all of what they knew was false. She said he had gone missing with valuable company property—intellectual and otherwise.

"What property?"

"I can't tell you that. I can tell you the name on his passport is Donovan Foley."

"Where have I heard that name," I said.

She had a request for me involving Foley. For some reason, his name evoked the sound of an elevator chime. I thought about the way people arranged their bodies in elevators, given the space available. I considered the field of Internet voyeurs (dozens if not scores) arranged in a grid of equidistant points, followed by the 3 X 3 schema of "slaves" in Grayson Blanco's portfolio. Three rows of three, with an empty room at the center of the formation: Donovan Foley's room. The name suggested a thought I couldn't manage to catch.

"The name is almost certainly a pseudonym," she said.

While I pondered this, Blanche mentioned that even the hints dropped by her boss, Reginald "Bob" Fister, CEO and Founder of Vector Industries, suggested an aura of mythology if not outright Space Opera surrounding Foley's nature and origins. She made a request that intrigued me.

"What do I get out of it?" I asked.

"A badge, access to the Control Room, a username. Any other resources you might need."

I puzzled over what she meant by "any other resources," then came to the realization that I had already decided to break into Donovan's house for my own purposes before asking what my reward would be.

12

Blanche escorted me out of the building, remaining behind to finish up a few tasks. She provided me with Foley's address, as well as instructions for proceeding from the end station to the address, instructions for entering the home, and a "guest badge" for returning to the Control Room whenever I desired. I had jitters coming on as I advanced to the subway. I took the train northwest, toward the line's final stop. It was a relief that Foley and I lived on separate lines, though I realized how illogical this was.

Intense discomfort began in the zone of my stomach and intestine, my abdominal muscles as tight or tighter than those of my face. The body is an unfortunate thing. After a few minutes, the discomfort's sway over my awareness retreated. I was not alone in the subway car, or I would have considered a desperate idea or two.

The recorded voice announced the end station, and I found myself wondering if the owners of various subway voices still lived, whether they took public transit, and what their ages were. Some were surely computer-generated, but others may have grown old riding the subway system, listening to a voice trapped in time while theirs grew gravelly and declined. How many people on earth have died listening to the sound of their own voice?

I exited and lingered on the platform, wanting the other riders to clear before I left. Who knew if any were Donovan's neighbors? I passed more than one liquor store and brake repair center before turning onto a side street

58

with an Integrated Wellness Yoga Garage on the corner. His house wasn't far.

Next to the yoga studio was what looked like an old paint shop, its dusty front windows displaying a work area filled with junk. Piles of rusted metal, rags, and stacks of cardboard boxes covered the entire back wall. On the corner of a workbench, seemingly posed, was a headless doll. The shop had the look of a cluttered Cornell box, complete with star charts and stuffed bird. A feeling grew in me that I was actually inside the dusty room, immobile and looking out, or that something inside the shop was aware of my presence, and had prepared the scene for my viewing pleasure. I considered whether Donovan owned this property as well, was its caretaker, or viewed it remotely. The headless doll in a ruffled dress seemed placed for a laugh.

Donovan's house was far enough from the station and city to have a yard, far enough to possess buffers from the nearly identical houses around it. As I began to cross the grass, an animal rounded the corner of the house and started trotting toward me.

I had entered the yard at its northeast corner; the dog had emerged from the house's rear (south side) and ran past me in a north by northeasterly direction. Blanche had informed me about the dog, saying it was small and friendly, and if not friendly, harmless, and if not harmless, not present. Lover of animals that I was, I tensed as the dog approached, prepared to speak kindly to it, and froze as the dog came into focus, or failed to. The dog that ran past had no face. The animal had appeared so low to the ground at least in part because its face was a blur—the dog's face, head, and neck entire could have been covered in a pet cone designed to display the background colors of the dog's present environment, rendered in a swirl.

I considered the possibility that Foley might have cameras on his property, wondered about cameras in neighboring houses, the CCTV systems of local businesses. The letters "CCTV" allow the phrase "closed-circuit television" to hide in plain sight, much like the cameras themselves. Like an ATM, or Kleenex. The longer I held the letters in my mind, the more they made me think of Russian characters, somehow. I tried to stop thinking, to stop worrying about cameras. I had likely been surveilled for years without a care, so why start now? I was locked in on a single path—the circuit was closed.

The dog was soon out of sight, and perhaps had never been there at all. Around the back I climbed the porch, its railings lined with spider plants. I tried the sliding glass door—locked. A screen covered in lumps of bugs—mostly dead though some still moving—budged, and I leaned it against the side of the house. The window gave, just as Blanche said it would. Gripping the inside of the window, I managed to get a leg up, lost it, adjusted my pants, pulled, and straddled the window-ledge. One leg and part of my torso were inside Donovan's home, specifically in a fairly modern bathroom of gray and dark marble.

The phrase "cone of shame" occurred to me, standing alone in the bathroom of a strange man's house, my smell filling the room. I smelled like my memory of my father, and became conscious of this thought in the form of a voiceover, something to the effect of: "There comes a time in every man's life—a time of change, a time of confusion, a time of desperation—when he detects an odor on himself that used to issue from his father's body." Clean sweat and cut grass, along with a hint of something else—Brylcreem?

I entered the hallway, checked both directions, stepped back into the bathroom, and closed the door. There was no way around it, unless I were to crawl out the window and shit outside. My bowels were hot and jumpy; I could nearly feel my heartbeat in there. The bowl was clean, though stained from a longtime mineral drip.

What followed was an event—or several small events, depending on one's point of view—that in my mind, speaking from a privileged position and lacking direct experience of the subject, could potentially rival at least a small percentage of human births by the metrics of pain and duration. Initially, nothing happened, as in the first moments of an effort to push a car out of mud.

I regulated my breathing, thinking "Now you're in for the long haul," and ruminated on mental images of the word "haul." Huskies hauling a sled up a fierce gradient, "hauling ass," commercial freighters hauling cargo, the ship in *Fitzcarraldo* being hauled up the mountain, and so on. When people talk about "involuntary sounds," they usually aren't sincere. I vowed to change my diet, to change everything.

I was grateful for the presence of liquid soap, as I wouldn't want to touch a bar used by Foley. Drying my hands on my shirt, I entered the hallway. Light brown carpet and wall sconces. Furniture in the living room was covered in dust cloths, except for a telescope supported by a tripod near the large front window, curtained to obscure any view into the house. Brushing the curtain aside revealed the lawn, street, and houses across the way. Active sprinklers, though no people, nor animals, in sight. I parted and released the edges of curtain flaps so that they allowed the telescope lens to peak through, but let little light into the room.

The view through the eyepiece was of the house across the street, namely its front and kitchen windows. The lights were on, though nothing of interest was happening. A hummingbird hovered by a feeder outside the kitchen, fleeing when a second razzed it. I wondered what Donovan observed from his perch. I walked into his kitchen, unprepared.

The liquids he bottled were many in kind, or at least that's how it looked at first. When I was younger I had tried to collect my saliva. It grew a mould before I could fill the bottle, every time. Donovan's kitchen was stacked. I didn't know what I was looking at. Juice, milk, spit, blood, soda, ether, urine? Airtight mason jars formed a second wall, covered counters, filled the cabinets I dared open, rested on a table made long by many leaves. Andres Serrano came to mind, though he was far from the only one. Cher Lloyd and Howard Hughes. Bottles and jugs across America, tossed out of big rig windows by long haul truckers and found along the interstates, the so-called Pee Bottle Corridors. The room was odorless, though filled with urine, the varying coloration of the samples likely determined by the specimen's age, and the diet, health, and hydration of the donor. Was this an art project revolving around bodily fluids, or evidence of some disorder? A piss archive, like any archive, becomes cloudier the farther back you go.

I hadn't touched a thing. I maneuvered through the kitchen, using what walking space was available. I pictured Foley making music with his moistened fingers, learning the sounds of each jar with its differing liquid levels. Stairs beside the pantry were a welcome discovery. I stopped in fascination to observe a red-orange goldfish swimming calmly in one of the jars. Or perhaps it was floating, and only appeared alive. Goldfish, despite their reputation, have a memory span of up to five months, and can easily outsmart a trout.

Bubbles emerged from the fish's mouth, perhaps programmed. I blinked, saw that every jar in the kitchen contained a fish, blinked, and saw only empty jars. I turned to the stairs and began to climb, each step seeming to increase the pressure on my head and chest cavity.

Upstairs the air was warm and stale. A bout of the spins came, then receded as my breathing slowed. The room was cramped and red, though like everything else, something was off. The color differed from the video I had observed—the red was deeper and the walls could have been freshly painted, or shellacked, they were so shiny. An item that hadn't been in the frame: another curtained window accompanied by telescope. Peeking through, I saw the westerly neighbor's yard and a single window opaque with blinds.

I had neglected to look inside Donovan's refrigerator.

The desk, the room's centerpiece, held little information. Touching the keyboard disturbed the screensaver, bringing up a password entry field. I wondered if Blanche was observing me now. I began to fear that something in the general vicinity of Donovan Foley's house—the air, a vibration, a frequency, some sort of inaudible, subliminal, post-hypnotic something-or-other—was affecting my brain.

I pictured Blanche watching me as I looked at the empty password field. She had no suggestions for passwords to try, and neither did I. She had in fact mentioned the unlikelihood of gaining access to any devices in the house. A list of passwords tried, with variations and without hope for success included: *foleydonovan, donovanfoley, goldfish, urinetrouble, highway40, mansonman, PanAm103, deserthole, hiddendrawer, orangehighwaytoheaven, pupfish.*

I froze, sweating, when I heard what sounded like a knot of wood exploding in a fire, or the house settling due to a shift in temperature, or a heavy foot on a stair. I waited for thirty seconds, two minutes, five. Hearing no further sounds, I walked with care to the stairway and looked down. No one there, as far as I could see.

The calendar I had previously spotted in the video feed had that day's date circled in red marker. A deadline of some sort? Dry cleaning? Perhaps Blanche would know what it meant. But would she reveal what she knew? I fantasized about her watching me from a remote location. My engagement in this mode of thinking was interrupted by a text from the subject of my reverie.

Blanche: Recommend you exit premises immediately

I took a closer look at the black leather desk chair, and noticed a black article of clothing draped over the back. It matched the color of the chair, and seemed to be a t-shirt. Had the t-shirt been there when I watched the video feed? Had someone been here in the interim? Was the t-shirt there when I entered the room even? Sweat continued its course.

On the way out, I found the downstairs bedroom, though bed, dresser, and bedside table were veiled by dust covers. The house was more safe house than house house. I lifted the cover off the bedside table, and nearly replaced it before noticing a business card. "Donovan Foley, Artist" was printed on the front, along with the name of a museum and a single word: *Glockengespenst.* On the back of the card was a symbol:

It was as though the previous shapes had continued to drift. The "o" or o-like shape had broken open, parts of it worn away to admit the "I" or vertical bar to its interior. It was as though a palatal plosive had been entered by the symbol for a dental click. I later discovered that the symbol on the back of Foley's card denoted, in mathematics, the set of all complex numbers, a term for a number expressed in two parts: real numbers and imaginary units. The Italian mathematician, inventor, scientist, and pathological gambler or ludomaniac Gerolamo Cardano, among others, was known to refer to imaginary numbers as "fictitious."

I left the house the way I came, closing the screen and bathroom window and walking back to the subway.

Rounding the corner of the house, my main concern was being spotted by a neighbor or by Foley himself. I doubted he talked to his neighbors much, though they were clearly on his mind.

A wave of starlings or blackbirds or the usual mass-traveling dark things poured out of a nearby field and continued in a nearly unbroken undulating mass for far longer than seemed possible. It turned out they were fleeing the sound of a distant helicopter, its rotor blades circulating while appearing still, a solid ring made by the revolving blades slicing through air so quickly that their image remained behind. A film projection of sorts.

The sound of a bell pulled me out of my head, and I saw a man in a brown suit approaching from behind on a bicycle. I edged off the sidewalk and onto grass, continuing to walk while repeatedly glancing back. His look was one I'd describe as "moustache-plus," and he was rocking BluBlockers. As he neared, the man in brown directed an unbroken stare in my direction, and rang his bell at roughly one-second intervals. I was tempted to push him off his bike, his head swiveling in my direction as he passed. There was no other traffic, human or vehicular, until I reached the station.

13

The Museum or Center or Institute or Space was either a brand new cube or a repurposed industrial hole. It looked the way you might expect: straight, clean lines; glass, steel, and concrete. Homage to the grid.

I paid to enter, clipped on a plastic item that signified my ticket, and took an elevator to a floor that could potentially contain *Glockengespenst*, whatever that might prove to be. In my experience, breezing through a gallery without seeming to pay attention indicates that a person knows either very little about the work, or a great deal. That is, people who don't look are unable to look or have already seen too much.

I tried to remember whether I had deleted my last password attempt at Foley's house, or whether I left it there? And what was it? In its familiarity, the phrase "Foley's house" sounded like a television show or the home of a frequently visited childhood pal. It brought to mind the popular song chorus consisting of the first-person plural possessive and the word for domicile, equidistant from the extremities, streetwise.

After making it most of the way through a traveling exhibition on abstraction and "the line," I stopped to rest on a bench. A guard entered the room, replacing another one standing in the corner. The ritual was: stationary guard observes approaching guard and vice versa, approaching guard arrives and becomes stationary, guards exchange brief greetings, guards optionally exchange one joke, formerly stationary guard rotates to next room. Their gazes implied they had seen everything as well.

On the bench, I considered the line and its erasure. Rauschenberg erasing De Kooning, for example, and the content of that gesture. The piece "worked" (if it worked) or was made possible because Rauschenberg owned the De Kooning drawing, or was given De Kooning's consent. But was consent required? I imagined an artist planning and executing an illegal conceptual piece in a museum space, one that would involve being charged with multiple counts of malicious destruction of property—as many counts as possible. Rauschenberg erasing De Kooning, but on steroids. Perhaps the artist would literally be on steroids. The artist should certainly train with weights (to increase strength for wielding a blunt implement) and at the track (to evade guards). There were other ways this might be taken to its logical conclusion.

After making my way to another level, I encountered the following wall text:

In German, a carillon is also called a Glockenspiel, while in French, the glockenspiel is often called a carillon. These are two distinct instruments.

A few paces later, I stood in front of the work titled "*Glockengespenst*," the piece I had come to find, the piece somehow linked to Donovan Foley. I continued reading.

MARGARET TUSSENVOEGSELS
Born 1948 in Erie, Pennsylvania; lives in New York
Glockengespenst, 2001
marble, Glock 17 pistol (non-firing replica)
Extended loan from Miriam and Roger Bevacqua

Glockenspiel is a musical instrument consisting of a set of tuned metal bars mounted in a frame and struck with small hammers. From the German, it literally means "bell play." The term Brockengespenst, or Brocken Spectre, refers to an optical phenomenon originally observed in the Brocken, a peak in Germany's Harz Mountains. The sight occurs in misty mountain regions when an observer's greatly magnified shadow is projected on clouds. As early as the 18th century, those who experienced the shadow effect were convinced they were seeing a ghost.

The work consisted of an unadorned white marble pedestal, a perfect rectangular prism roughly three feet high, on top of which rested a Glock nine-millimeter, the 9x19mm so-called Parabellum series. Around the pedestal were four stanchions supporting a knee-height rope. Standing a few strides away was a guard who paced, or slid a phone out of his pocket just enough to check the time.

The pedestal was a tiny rectangular monolith inside a square of rope inside the white cube of a room, itself inside the cube of the museum space. I watched two families move in opposing orbits around the piece before I stepped into a small dark room containing a video projector. On the screen was an older man wearing a silver wig, sitting up in bed, and talking to someone off-camera.

Old Man: Oh yes, they've always been around.

Person off-camera: I wonder what they're like.

OM: They're different. Walking in other people's bodies. They're called walk-ins.

POC: What do they look like?

With the families gone, I shared the space around
Glockengespenst with two others, including the guard. The
pistol stood out as if in relief, as if carved into the marble
and painted black. A man I hadn't noticed approached the
sculpture. He was wearing a brown suit, and had orange-
tinted sunglasses resting on his head. I realized this was
the man on bicycle earlier, the one ringing the bell and
staring at me as he passed.

What happened next happened the way things tend to
happen—quickly. The man in the brown suit stepped over
the rope barrier around the piece, triggering a brief alarm
composed of a single, deep tone. The guard reacted by
stepping forward and raising an arm, repeating variations
of "excuse me," "please step back," and "you can't be in
there." In an effort to get closer to the man in the brown
suit, the guard circled the piece, but the man kept the
mini-monolith between them.

The guard radioed for assistance as the man in the
brown suit removed a putty knife from his pocket and
shoved it under the gun. Having broken through adhesive
in at least one spot, he grabbed the barrel and pulled, using
the grip as leverage. A pop was heard, and the gun was in
his hand. Later I would be sure that the eyes of the man
in the brown suit briefly took me in over the monolith. He
pushed a button on the pistol's side and the magazine slid
out with an oiled click. He retrieved a glinting object from
his mouth, stuck it into the clip, and inserted the clip
until the sound of the click bounced around the room's
high ceiling and cement floor. He pulled the slide back,

released it, stuck the gun in his mouth, and pulled the trigger.

My reaction to the black metal object, or the black plastic object (the Glock has a polymer frame), was a thought resembling "there's no problem" but expressed as a single idea. An internal shrug. There was absolutely no way the gun in the mouth of the brown-suited man would fire. The wall text said so. Logic said so. Any item brought into a museum had to be approved by a legal team, the curator and curatorial department, the director, the board of trustees, et al. The idea that a potentially lethal weapon could be legally displayed in a gallery frequented by upwards of 2000 people in a 24-hour period was ludicrous. It would be uninsurable. It would be irresponsible. It would be unconscionable. For a host of reasons, including the most obvious to all monitoring the situation, it would be a bad idea to leave a functioning gun, even unloaded and glued to marble, out in the open. Perhaps if it were under glass, the glass secured with screws so that, should they be tampered with—by a black-masked team with power drills for example—the sound would be sufficient to raise the alarm in time, though a locking mechanism would be advisable. At any rate, the Glock that should be under glass, or plexiglass, was labeled as a non-firing replica, which meant nothing could be done as far as alteration that would make it firable. Gaston Glock, founder of the Glock firearms company, designer, plastics expert, and entrepreneur, was born in 1929. At age 81 he married Kathrin Tschikhof, who was born in 1980. Gaston, one of the friendliest-sounding names imaginable.

Blood and other thicker stuff came out in a spray,

leaving specks on the 18-foot ceiling. The former man in the brown suit slumped down, his weight stretching the rope barrier and upending two of the stanchions' metal bases. A concentrated deeper red coated the pedestal and the floor around it. The guard said something. It looked like years had dropped from his face. Had any been added to mine? The guard's voice trembled when he spoke again, saying we should clear the area, that people were on the way.

Soon I was answering questions in a conference room on another floor. They didn't suspect me of anything, nor was there anything to suspect really. Not exactly true. I gave my name and contact information, claimed I had never seen the victim (and perpetrator?) before he put a bullet in his head. Suicide by firearm is the most successful method, and the most common, in the United States. The officer who questioned me couldn't release the name of the man in the brown suit, but said I could find out in the paper. My mind was on the business card in my pocket, and the fear of some connection being made between me and the suicide. When I considered the triviality of possessing a business card with the name of a work in front of which a man had killed himself, everything struck me as a bit absurd.

14

Much later, alone in my silent apartment, I could hear the shell casing hit the floor, an echo from earlier. I heard all the sounds, had been hearing them repeat for some time: the pop, the click, the click, the click, the collision of metal with bone and flesh, the sound of something wet, the sound of two men breathing. It isn't terribly uncommon for a disturbed individual to enter a museum for the purpose of defacing a work, but I couldn't recall any instances of self harm with a weapon. An Internet search for "museum suicide" returned the following suggestions:

tate museum suicide
hirshhorn museum suicide
liverpool museum suicide
bc museum suicide
british museum suicide
guggenheim museum suicide
kelvingrove museum suicide

In the case of the Tate, a visitor jumped to his death from a balcony. The Hirshhorn suicide was a museum guard who shot himself with his service revolver in a basement level locker room. Liverpool witnessed a case of murder-suicide—a man stabbed a woman before falling 35 feet, also from a balcony. In an office inside the Royal British Columbia Museum, a curator committed suicide with a shotgun. At the British Museum was another jumper. The Guggenheim suicide refers to a life-sized model of Pinocchio, a marionette made of resin, steel, and epoxy paint, floating facedown in a reflecting pool. The incident at Kelvingrove, it turns out, was merely a case of career suicide.

A surprising number of documentaries exist on the subject of Russian roulette, the most notable titled *Schrödinger's Bullet*. Many of these films, online and on DVD, are fake, and parts of the aforementioned surely are. Whether *Schrödinger's Bullet* should be classified as a snuff film is uncertain; it is illegal in the US (though it can be mailed from out of country for a fee, like anything). The film quality is rough, the footage seemingly cobbled together from many different cameras. The first three minutes are a montage of clicks, single pulls of the trigger across the geographic and socio-cultural spectrum. Usually the man—it is almost always a young male—is alone, occasionally he is surrounded by a rowdy crowd giving encouragement. A bearded man with pudgy cheeks and thinning hair stares into the camera, produces the revolver, spins it: CLICK. The colon: the barrel: that from which issues forth. A wiry man with gang tattoos: CLICK. A backwoods gathering around a bonfire: CLICK. A solitary man on a West Elm couch: CLICK. A sweaty man against a bathroom wall: CLICK. A solemn girl in pajamas: CLICK. A drunken man at a barbecue: CLICK. A man in a room: CLICK. A man in a room: CLICK. A man in a suit: CLICK. A man in a tank top: CLICK. A soldier: CLICK. An accountant: CLICK. A smuggler: CLICK. A teenager: CLICK. A magician: CLICK. A man in a room: CLICK. An addict: BOOM.

The first casualty, if it really is one, leaves red on a

white wall. The structure of the film continues in this way. Players escape unscathed for minutes on end, to the point where boredom may even threaten the tension. Then a purported death occurs. The players who win are never shown again, nor is more than one attempt shown. Rarely does the film depict a player actually loading the gun, raising the obvious question. When anyone speaks it is in English, Spanish, Russian, Chinese, something else. The footage skews toward the war-torn.

The credits listed the film company as one called Phobic Films, though I was unable to find evidence of any company incorporated under that name. The film was also interspersed with interview footage, short clips from Russian roulette players and survivors, one with brain damage. "Roulette" is from Latin via the French, originating in "rota," which is Latin for "wheel." Clear implications. More than one purported survivor admitted to addictions: smoking, alcohol, hard drugs, sex, gambling, even Russian roulette itself. The game provided the usual stimulation: a buzz, a rush, a thrill, euphoria. Some claimed the pleasure was in the anticipation (the loading, the spinning) while others felt release upon hearing the click. One player said he got an erection while loading the gun, masturbated, and timed his orgasm to coincide with pulling the trigger. Another said he tended to lose control of his bowels out of nervousness. Someone with a graduate degree said they played to cope with the pain of existence, or something to that effect.

One extended montage of many near misses and one hit was accompanied by a theme song soundtrack from the popular board game:

I could never find a copy of the film, but watched it more than once with friends. At some point it became obvious that this documentary was influenced as much by cinema as reality. If it was real life, the subjects were performing it. I spent a lot of time thinking about the rhythm of the phrase "Russian roulette." When holding barrel to temple, how many suicides or would-be suicides had *The Deer Hunter* on their mind?

Smack in the middle of *Schrödinger's Bullet* is its most disturbing offering. A man wearing a black balaclava is sitting at a solid oak table, bare except for a revolver and a single round. The camera zooms in on delicate hands. The man grips the pistol, flicks his wrist to open the cylinder, inserts a round, and spins the cylinder. The camera slowly pans out until the frame contains the table and chair from the floor up, and the man's whole body. He places the gun to his head. Muzzle flash as the loaded chamber discharges, and the man slides to the floor. No blood is visible, however. The camera zooms in on the head, distended to an extreme degree, stretching the balaclava as though a pumpkin were inside.

Near the film's final moments, one is treated to a scene billed as "The World's Longest Continuous Russian Roulette Competition." A referee announces the last two contestants are approaching the 36-minute mark. As remarkable as this may sound, there are a few reasons it isn't beyond the realm of possibility. Consider, for the moment, that the world record for Number of Correct Consecutive Coin Flip Guesses currently stands at 19. Further consider that the coin in question was a commemorative Kennedy half-dollar, first minted in 1964.

The two players had developed a rhythm that was mesmerizing. They faced one another, eyes locked, with the referee to one side. Simultaneous spins were followed by a moment's pause after both cylinders had come to rest. Both raised revolvers to heads, pulled triggers, generated clicks. A metronome-like pattern: spin-pause-lift-CLICK, spin-pause-lift-CLICK, spin-pause-lift-CLICK, spin-pause-lift-CLICK, spin-pause-lift-CLICK. It could have been ballet.

Do you suppose this went on forever? Do you suppose one of the players turned his gun on the other, only to have it click and be disqualified if not jailed, executed? Do you suppose a player turned his gun on the other and managed to hit a loaded chamber? Do you suppose both players turned their guns on the referee, who happened to be armed, and managed to score double clicks before being gunned down? Do you suppose both players managed to shoot the referee before escaping into the Ural Mountains? Do you suppose both players hit loaded chambers at the same time, in what would be a 1 in 36 chance, fulfilling their suicide pact?

A point of order: the odds of actually firing a round can be far less than one in six.

If the cylinder is allowed to come to rest in an upright revolver, gravity causes the loaded, and therefore heaviest, chamber to skew towards bottom.

<h1 style="text-align:center">15</h1>

I spent the entire weekend holed up in my apartment, had the day off on Monday, and called in sick on Tuesday to continue the stretch. I had discovered what I wanted to do with my future, or at least the immediate part of it. The website dedicated to the oeuvre of Lucian Bevacqua had assumed a central role, particularly those short films featuring Donovan Foley. I found myself caught up in the intensely competitive game of scouring the Internet for "rare" Bevacqua films or film clips, the difference between which was often difficult to spot. The director's work tended toward the fragmentary, but fragments of some larger fragment that felt vastly oblique and powerful.

Gould performing Brahms's *Ten Intermezzi for Piano* played on a loop for the longest time. When even I couldn't stand the repetition, I acquired a copy of Wagner's *Ring* cycle—not for its sonic properties, but because of the shape it suggested, and because it was a cycle. The more I listened, the more I searched online, the more I began to think of even myself as an interlude of sorts, a loop.

One of my favorite works by Bevacqua was called *Members of Congress in Bondage*. The film was purportedly only available for sale to private collectors, and had never been screened, though it popped up on a video sharing site briefly, only to be inexplicably removed. Others were shared over social media, uploaded to video streaming sites, or offered as digital downloads on obscure websites with domains like .ch (Switzerland), .na (Namibia), .ru (Russia), .mil (US military), and .film. I downloaded, catalogued, and shared with my newfound online community, earning cred and literal points for my contributions. I felt like a star.

Another favorite of mine was a brief film called *Notes from the Zero*. It featured Foley, or someone who dressed like him, with face likewise pixelated. He sat against a gray wall, speaking at length in a distorted voice about his favorite number. Zero, if you couldn't guess. The number zero had a rounded, if not purely circular aspect, and therefore a kind of fullness. Its emptiness, according to Foley, was also the most beautiful thing about it. The word "zero" contains an "o," a more perfect loop. Its initial "z," too, suggests a certain finality. As Foley spoke, I was overcome by a deep sadness. By the end of the film, I could relate to him completely.

The most powerful Bevacqua film I encountered on that long weekend, however, was called *The Prism*. As I watched, the now-familiar dizziness—the spins—crept over me. The film consisted of quick cuts: cityscapes, subway encounters, rooftop shots, street traffic, and intimate apartment views, all cobbled together from surveillance footage. As the spins ratcheted up, I felt something else that I could only describe as intense longing. I was in the presence of great art, created from the everyday, and I wanted more of it.

16

Blanche summoned, and I didn't delay. By the time I stood in front of the Vector building, I assumed my approach had been tracked and catalogued. Then again, maybe no one cared, or the resources were directed elsewhere. Blanche met me in the lobby, and handed me a plastic ID badge that would grant me Control Room access.

When asked about my emotional state, I said the museum incident still seemed unreal. She declined to explain how she knew about the man in the brown suit.

"You've never seen a man die before," she said.

"Not a man," I said. "Not violently."

"A woman?"

"I've been in the room when it happened," I said.

She asked to see my badge, and when I obliged, turned it over to reveal a digital display I hadn't noticed. It currently read "8."

"To get to Control, you go up before going down, Heraclitus. You'll remember it is Level -3. The badge will display the recommended route, since access shifts almost constantly."

Blanche said her superior would like to interview me, if I had time.

Swallowing became difficult, or I became aware of a difficulty pre-existing my awareness. The idea that I would be interviewed, even debriefed, by one of the higher-ups at Vector caused a brief and inexplicable panic to recur. I planned to ask questions of my own, but if Blanche's boss was no more forthcoming than Blanche, I might as well ask the entrails of a bird.

The secretary working for Reginald "Bob" Fister, CEO and Founder of Vector Industries, motioned Blanche and I toward a number comfortable seating options. Leather and chrome on steel. It wasn't long before Fister emerged to the tune of Jean-Joseph Mouret's *Suites de symphonies*, the one heavy on trumpet, timpani, and violin, the one better known as the theme to a long-running dramatic television series of lofty (one supposes) cultural cachet.

Fister, wearing a gray suit, looked younger than I had expected. He waved me inside. Our movement into his office could have taken place on a conveyor belt or moving walkway, our rates of speed identical. He practically floated backwards around his desk into the space in front of his chair as I trailed behind in a similar fashion, the door closing behind us without sound. He asked me to sit, and did the same. "Travelator" was the word I wanted. In fact, travelators, escalators, and similar machines were a kind of giant loop—walk long enough and your steps would begin to repeat themselves.

Fister appeared normal enough, but I couldn't get a read on him. The longer I looked, the younger he seemed. Brown hair with gel in it (not too much), an almost-smile that didn't waver. The energy of the room was one of turbines great in number concentrated in the person of Bob Fister. Whatever the flow, whether water, steam, gas, energy, air, or something else entirely, it was running through Fister. It was impossible for me to conceive of him as "Reginald." Clean-shaven, gray suit, a ring. At first I assumed it was a college ring, though looking closer revealed a symbol at odds with the logos of any alma maters of which I was aware.

Ɔ

Again, a connection to previous symbols was apparent, though the logic of their transformations escaped me. I should clarify that the symbol on Fister's ring appeared as such from my vantage point, meaning it would be flipped from the perspective of the wearer. Not exactly a reverse "c," the letter was closer to a broken "o," broken zero, or set of pincers closing in on negative space. It could have been a Claudian letter, one of three introduced into the Roman alphabet by emperor Claudius, this one known as an "antisigma." The only detectable pattern in the symbols I continued to encounter was one of diminution, hollowing out, breaking apart—a pattern of drift.

It was difficult to find purchase on Fister's face, though not in the same way as Foley's. The face of the CEO was smooth, tanned, and clean-shaven, though less in the sense of "hair cut by lubricated metal" than the sense of "follicles destroyed with pulses of light from lasers."

He seemed relaxed in a way that relaxed me, before I wondered if I was undergoing hypnosis. I was opposed to being hypnotized, which I was given to understand would ward off the hypnotic state. Perhaps the truism was inaccurate, misinformation spread by hypnotists. Fister had a face I would remember as a collection of colors and lines.

"I'm sorry for what happened in the museum," he said.

When I made the ritualistic remark that it was no fault of his, Fister responded that Vector Industries, unfortunately and off the record, was not without fault.

"The man who shot himself." he said. "He did so under the persuasive powers of someone you might know."

"Foley," I said.

"Yes. Persuasion, coercion, another kind of nudge."

I asked how Foley, how anyone, could sway a person to suicide, and what he meant by "nudge." Meaningful elaboration was beyond my expectations. I asked why Foley wanted the man in the brown suit to pull the trigger, though I suspected the answer.

"A hostile gesture, a desperate gesture, intended to scare you off," Fister said.

In the office was a door behind the desk, mirroring the door we had entered. The corner of the office featured a large animal, stuffed and erect, one that is illegal to possess in the US, at least in this century.

It was difficult to look away from Fister's folded hands and single ring. Not on the ring finger, not on the left hand. A single black stone—obsidian? Gold, white gold, platinum, wrought iron, ultrium? I considered the Fisherman's Ring, and the idea of kissing it. Piscatory. Where did the door behind the desk lead, I didn't ask.

"Why am I involved?" I asked.

"Let me answer your question with one, if I may," he said. "What can we offer you?"

"I don't understand."

Fister rose and began to pace, assuming an almost performative mode.

"Vector Industries has significant resources. An amount in an account, cash in a briefcase, whatever—we can give you this. Access to information, this we can provide. Something else, something more tangible, corporeal..." He paused, expression however unchanged.

"What are you suggesting?"

"I'm not suggesting so much as stating that Vector is poised to provide you with a key, so to speak, to rooms housing untold wonders, living and otherwise."

"We need Donovan," Fister said. "We need what he knows, the company property in his possession, what was stolen from us. Do you think you'd be willing to assist us? What would persuade you to do so?"

"Let me ask you a direct question."

"Please."

"What exactly is the issue with Donovan's face? What am I seeing, and what causes the distortion?"

Fister's expression was closer to changing than ever before.

"You seem tired," he said. "What I can tell you: Donovan is what you could call a consummate blender. Maybe he was born with it, maybe it's Maybeline."

I stood and walked behind the desk, Fister's body turning in the swivel chair so that his face followed my progress. The door opened and shut behind me as before, and I found myself face to face with Fister, somehow, again. The next room appeared identical: a door behind me, a door behind the desk, window, desk, chair, seated human, large mounted exotic vertebrate.

"By blender I mean one who blends in, not the appliance, you understand," this version of Fister said.

When I asked what else he could tell me, Fister said that the current world population was only 5-10% of the number of humans who had ever lived, and that this percentage would only decrease, ipso facto.

Standing, I paced the room, examining the corners for some kind of seam, or a flap I could pull to reveal or create a rift. I circled the stuffed vertebrate, then passed through the door behind Fister.

This time he was drinking tea, or drinking something out of a teacup. The room and furniture were the same— only the teacup differed. The door closed behind me without sound.

"Bone china," Fister said. "Very white, nearly translucent. This cup is high in phosphate—well over thirty percent—obtained from animal bone and other sources. The bone content, I want to stress, is animal in origin. Bone ash."

"What can you tell me about Donovan Foley?"

"Not much, unfortunately. Our records, meager though they are, hold a passport that may be falsified. Donovan Foley, son of Miriam and Roger Foley, born in July of 1969. Born near (but not in) a little town called Lebanon, Kansas, off of U.S. Route 281, the offspring of U.S. Route 81. Route 281 runs from North Dakota to Texas, stopping just short of the Canadian and Mexican borders, and is 1,872 miles long. The salient fact about Lebanon, Kansas is its designation as the closest town to the Geographic Center of the Contiguous United States. Foley has worked for us since 1999. It has come to our attention that his work history preceding that time is completely fabricated."

As Fister sipped from his china cup, I noticed a marking on the bottom, a symbol I had expected, dreaded, and possibly longed for. The same symbol, in fact, that had been on his ring (the ring having since disappeared). Fister threw a folder onto the desk in front of me, a manila one bulging with old photographs, newspaper and magazine clippings, photocopied documents, reports, a small packet. There were no photos of Donovan Foley.

"Those are for later," Fister said, as I perused the folder.

"What is it you want me to do?"

"Take a few days to think it over. There's a packet inside with two envelopes—one for you to open, one to leave closed unless you wish to terminate our agreement before it begins. The first envelope contains a contract. The second envelope is something we'd like delivered."

"To Foley."

"Yes."

"Like a subpoena."

"Very much like a subpoena, yes."

When I opened the door to the next office, I found myself unable to follow through on my plan, which was to look back and verify the presence, within my sight range, of two Fisters at once. Pausing in the entryway, I felt increasing pressure on my head and torso, coupled with overwhelming fear of what was behind me, the fear experienced when leaving a basement by the stairs, back turned to an emptiness that may or not be empty.

The next room was nearly identical to the last, its changes minute, barely discernable. The teacup was no longer present, the carpet's edge extended slightly further into unexplored territory, and was it a deeper shade of red?

Fister's visage looked fresh, newly minted, though deciding if it differed from earlier iterations was equivalent to the familiar exercise at the optometrist. I recalled reading studies that shed light on the phenomenon of entering a room and immediately forgetting why one entered. It was the doorway. The change in environment involved in crossing the threshold of a doorway caused the brain to shift gears, to clear itself. Houses and doors: technologies of forgetting.

This next office must be the last. Fister held an ornamental folding fan at what could have been called a saucy angle, i.e. between 40 and 65 degrees. His face was somehow pinker. I picked up the folder and retraced my steps, moving from repeating room to repeating room, unsure if I passed through more offices on the way back than I had originally been through, or if I had taken a turn in one of the rooms and branched off into another series of offices without realizing it, the light a little different this time. In what would turn out to be the penultimate office before reaching the reception area, Fister confessed that the stuffed baboon was fake.

17

In the Control Room, I watched a man on one of the monitors, reading an online news article over his shoulder. It stated: "[illegible] had been held in a network of tents, sheds, and tarps in a 'hidden backyard-within-a-backyard' in Cedar Vale, Kansas." Who knew where I could find Blanche. I had the urge to leave town, to get on the road in a stolen vehicle and trade it for others multiple times until the trail went cold, but I had no destination in mind. I couldn't recall having stolen anything of value—not because I was morally opposed or lacked the nerve, but because I didn't see the point. I wondered whether I'd be capable of such a course of action.

The custom program Vector used was searchable by address. The address of the building I was in yielded multiple feeds, though none on my current floor, or on Fister's. Among the lobby feeds, I found one displaying the door I had used to enter the building. I scrolled back, watched myself enter the lobby on repeat. Time had gotten away from me.

Typing the address of Blanche's apartment yielded several matches, including a few nearby. One view was footage from the interior of a market: its aisles, exits, and stock room. Closer in was the view from a security camera behind her building, placed to monitor a fenced-in area containing a dumpster, a bike-rack, and a powerful motorcycle—a lime green and ebony Kawasaki. A Brahms *intermezzo* popped into my head, ceased, returned.

Much of this footage was incredibly mundane. I did,

however, recognize one feed as the interior of Blanche's apartment, her desktop computer's affixed webcam the likely source. Her bed was there, her bookshelves were there, her window, naturally, was there. The curtain didn't move in any sort of breeze. The curtain didn't move in a way that suggested a form behind it, thankfully, since that is one of the most potentially frightening sights, and would have been especially so in this case.

I closed the live feed of Blanche's apartment and found a menu item marked "History." Its options were arrayed as follows: 1d, 3d, 1w, 2w, 1m, 3m, 6m, 1y, 3y, 5y, 10y, max.

I clicked on "3d," signifying the last three days of footage, and watched the video player's long dark bar slowly fill with red, barely seeming to move. I didn't know what I hoped for—that's not exactly true. What I hoped for entailed Blanche returning from the gym, tossing shirt and gym shorts and sports bra into the hamper, perhaps missing with the shorts and bending over to retrieve them, slower than was necessary, Blanche in a towel, with a towel on her head, seated at her makeup station and applying lotion, frying rasher upon rasher of turkey bacon and yelping when the sizzling fat splattered, stretching, doing yoga in a black and green ensemble that matched her Kawasaki, reading for hours, supine on her sumptuous couch, phone to her ear and knees in the air, busying herself with papers and a small amount of plant material, rolling her own in a visual echo of Jennifer Lopez in *The Cell*. I essentially hoped for an endless succession of cliché fantasy, though rather than "hope" I meant "wistfully entertained without foresight or hope for actualization."

What I didn't hope for, skipping ahead three-quarters into the footage, was for Liam to walk into the picture. That dear friend of mine. To be clear, this turn of events did not establish anything like a "triangle," nor even arouse anything close to jealousy. I wasn't disappointed, I was perplexed. I watched Liam arrive, embrace Blanche, and join her on the couch. How the two of them knew each other I couldn't fathom. I was glued to footage of Liam and Blanche, Blanche and Liam, drinks in the kitchen, adding ice, liquor, herbs, garnishes, grinding nutmeg, carrying small plates to her coffee table, picking at food, chatting until their heads drifted together and remained close. They were both wearing shirts with buttons, it turned out. Soon Blanche was leading him by the hand into a dark place off camera. The reason buttons on clothing are invested with erogenous power is because they point to access. A shirt is just a shirt, whereas buttons provide a series of focal points or entryways. Pressure builds within the system just as each button disengages from its point of contact with fabric. Its release is gradual like the sluice of a lock.

I wanted to believe I had seen only what Blanche wanted me to see. As an employee of Vector, she likely knew (or selected) what was recorded in her home. She had also just given me access. The only way to proceed was as though Blanche knew what I knew. What did Liam and I have in common? Clearly, we had both attended a screening of *Pupfish*, Liam having informed me of the film's existence in the first place. Anything Blanche desired from Liam, I decided, revolved around the film, or his knowledge concerning its director. It seemed unlikely, though not impossible, that Blanche met Liam through random channels, or had known him for some time. It seemed impossible.

Knowing that Blanche could observe my viewing habits at any time, could be observing me even then, I steered clear of footage of her—compromising, titillating, mundane. Instead I viewed the highlights of a 3-month period in Liam's uneventful life. I watched him eat in front of his monitor, floss in front of his monitor, and I skipped forward when he reclined and got a certain glint in his eye. I wondered how often I simply stared, how often lost time took hold of me. I watched Liam put together the beginnings of an elaborate model train set in his bedroom before something lit up a corner of my brain. I felt a strangely painful sensation. I had dismissed the idea that Blanche and Liam (Liam and Blanche) were acquainted before the film encounter. But what if Liam had known all along? What if he worked for Vector in some capacity? What if he, in cahoots with Blanche, had set up my meeting with Donovan Foley? If not set up, then perhaps Vector had been monitoring Foley—through airport cameras, the black box, CCTVs—until a bystander's behavior indicated he or she saw something unusual. But what was Liam's role? I hoped my friend's involvement was limited and short-lived, for purely selfish reasons.

When a mosquito flew close to my face, I had to question whether it was another camera. A vehicle of drugs or disease? I clapped and blew its body off my palm, wiping hands on jeans. There was no blood inside. I wondered where it had incubated, where it had hatched. Where it could live in an office building.

18

When I next heard from Blanche, I was immersed in an online search for one of Bevacqua's rare creations, a love story of sorts called *Friendly Fire*. The film was a split-screen affair that tracked the movements of two strangers—a man and a woman—as they went about their business for one year in the same city. Though initially unknown to one another, the film depicts the two strangers shopping at the same grocery store, strolling through the same neighborhood, watching the same television shows alone in their separate apartments. The film culminates in a series of encounters in which the two become more than strangers, more than friends.

Unfortunately, every file I downloaded of the film turned out to be pure static. I had to give up for the moment, but did locate another Bevacqua offering called *Faces of Gaddafi*, assembled out of the five known mobile phone videos of the dictator's final moments. Artful, slow-motion repetitions of Gaddafi emerging from a drain, walking down a hill, touching his head wound, and staring at his bloody fingers in confusion. I read on a number of fan sites that Bevacqua became obsessed with footage of Gaddafi's death after learning that Vladimir Putin had reportedly become fixated on the footage as well, watching it over and over with the fear that he would be the next to go. On both counts, I could understand completely.

Blanche's voice was oddly friendly on the phone. She wanted to arrange a meeting. By this time, I had examined the contents of the folder given to me by Fister. The documents were visually unremarkable: an envelope marked "Foley" that was sealed along each edge with clear packing tape and opaque when held up to the light; an envelope marked "communiqué" that contained a list of three phrases, phrases purportedly belonging to three locations.

Blanche buzzed me up, and I climbed the stairs to her apartment. Her roommate, again, was nowhere to be seen. Her cat, again, was nowhere to be seen. She was wearing a black t-shirt featuring white lettering. When I showed her the documents, she asked whether I was tempted to open the Foley envelope.

I told her I was tempted, but not tempted enough. I had a feeling the envelope was some kind of test of loyalty, of my resolve. When I asked about the other document, she said it was a list of places where I'd be likely to encounter Donovan Foley. I looked at the list again.

Willow (Weeping)

Erebus

Baths (Russian and Turkish)

The phrase "weeping willow" rotated in my mind. I happened to know that the onetime moniker of the Grand Duke George Alexandrovich (a Romanov) was "the Weeping Willow." Apparently he cried a great deal.

"Have you ever seen Donovan Foley in real life?" I asked.

"Once," she said.

I asked what he looked like, and she said like a middle-aged businessman.

"It was a few months ago, as I was stopping by Fister's

office. A man was leaving when I arrived who, let's just say, made an impression," she said.

"What kind of impression?"

"You know the feeling when you see someone for the first time—a stranger—and you can immediately tell what kind of person they are? Trustworthy, shifty, what-have-you? Foley exuded incredible power. Particularly the eyes."

"What did his face look like to you?" I asked.

"A normal face belonging to a human. Nothing like your case."

I asked, in jest, whether Foley had turned her on.

"Not like Ted Bundy," she said.

I asked what she knew about Lucian Bevacqua, not expecting to be illuminated to any significant degree.

"He's harder to find than Foley, if you can believe it," she said.

"What's the connection between the two?"

She said that before Foley joined Vector Industries, and possibly after, he was an associate of Bevacqua's. Bevacqua used him in several films, all limited release. Though initially thought to be an employee of Bevacqua's, Foley's appearances were more like cameos. He may have actually helped fund a number of the productions.

"How old is Bevacqua?"

"In his 70s, though he's vigorous."

When Blanche described the Weeping Willow as "a bagnio covered with the veneer of an expensive restaurant," I said I was willing to scratch its surface. The suggestion that I bring a friend gave her pause, doubly so when I suggested Liam. It was, in fact, the first time I had seen an expression approaching surprise on her face.

My reasoning: what could it hurt? (Or was my reasoning something else entirely?) Since Blanche had brought Liam into the picture without my knowledge, this would perhaps restore a sort of balance, force Blanche's hand, or demonstrate that I wasn't completely predictable. Another hope of mine was that Liam would talk.

"You haven't signed a confidentiality agreement," she said. "But it would be wise to behave as if you had."

I was forbade from divulging any information about Donovan Foley or Vector Industries, especially the latter's surveillance capabilities. Briefing Liam would require subtlety worthy of Fister himself. The good news was Vector would be footing the bill.

19

A black SUV stretched to the length of three normal black SUVs arrived for me the following evening. I climbed in and greeted the driver, who raised the soundproof partition as if in response. I felt disappointed by his lack of headgear. The spacious seating area held a fleet of crystal glasses, a well-stocked bar, a polished counter lit by neon on either side of the vehicle, a mirrored ceiling, a sink with running water, a telephone, and either the stuffed baboon from Fister's office or its double. Two black garment bags containing suits were hanging in the back. In the pocket of the suit intended for me I came across a blindfold.

I selected a bottle of mezcal from the varieties on display, poured, and took a sip. Holding the bottle up to the light revealed a slowly revolving worm. Though mezcal and tequila are often conflated, the latter is a specific variety of the former, and it is only mezcal that can sometimes be found *con guso*, that is, "with worm."

This conflation owes much to the film *Poltergeist II: The Other Side* (1986), namely the iconic scenes in which Steve Freeling ingests a "tequila worm" that grows inside him until erupting in exquisitely horrific fashion. The worm, a vector for one Reverend Kane, possesses Freeling's body as a result of his penchant for drinking an entire bottle of tequila, *con guso*. Freeling's behavior, remarkably alert after polishing off the fifth, also serves as a thinly veiled critique of the dangers of alcoholism (lust, violence, incoherence) and a literalization of one's "inner demons."

I took a sip of mezcal. A comedic routine: What's the deal with things growing inside the body that is simply the worst? I'd prefer a broken leg to a tapeworm, whatever its size.

Before arranging the Weeping Willow operation, Blanche asked me if I had ever paid for sex. She may have asked if I had "been with a prostitute," a gentler question. Paying for sex (here's some sex) versus paying for time with a person, a stranger. No, she asked if I had ever visited a brothel. I told her I hadn't, which was true. The place I had visited didn't look like a brothel to me; it looked like a stranger's apartment.

A flashback:

The woman who approached me outside the bar said something like, "How'd you like a bit of fun?" or "Want some company, dreamboat?" Her name was Amber or Crystal or Bailey or Eve or Rain or Kira or Andromeda, maybe. I told her "no thanks," and watched her walk away. She did an over-the-shoulder hair toss and watched me watch her walk away. I decided to follow her. It's funny, psychology. I followed Rain, Eve, et al., for I don't remember how long. At some point, she noticed, and turned around grinning.

"Change your mind?" she asked, pressing her body against me. She was wearing at least one article of leather clothing. She claimed to live nearby, which I took to mean that she conducted business nearby in a shared apartment. The apartment, or the building itself, was likely owned by Candy or Andromeda's employer, who likely employed someone else to watch her from a window above, ever ready to direct violence at anyone who threatened his livelihood.

Bailey and I agreed on a transaction; Kira led me to an apartment building and up stairs while my stomach churned out acid. Once on the other side of a door in a pink-lit room, Amber asked me for the cash. Her demeanor changed; she told me to take off my pants and handed me a rough white hand-towel. I unfolded the towel and placed it on the bed, sitting down with my pants around my ankles.

"All the way off," she said. Crystal gripped me in one hand, asking "Have you been drinking?"

"You saw me come out of a bar," I said.

She asked if taking off her shirt would help matters. She said my hands were too cold, instructed me to warm them on my body.

"Not my nipples," she said. "They're too sore."

End flashback.

We arrived at Liam's apartment building, and the driver idled while I watched the metal gate out front, sipping mezcal. Memories of telling Kira "thanks," that I "had a nice time," maybe even that I "wished her the best" floated in my awareness before disintegrating.

Liam approached, letting the metal gate slam behind him. He crossed in front of the vehicle and paused by the driver's window. I could hear them speaking in low tones. I pressed the power window switch to no avail. While I considered contacting the driver to unlock my window button, Liam crossed in front of the car again, and entered the seating area.

We exchanged greetings as the stretch SUV started moving. I poured mezcal into a snifter, and Liam asked if I could find a white wine glass instead. Indulging him, I rummaged in bar cabinets until I found one. I felt a sense of dread building, unconnected to Liam, to our destination, but rather to the idea that this was all being filmed in some way, that I would be judged based on my performance.

"What were you discussing with the driver?" I asked.

"I wanted to make sure this was the right car. Other than that, just being friendly."

We opened garment bags and changed into the matching suits Vector had provided. I wondered how our measurements had been acquired. Body scans? Records of purchases from clothing stores? Size information entered for online purchases? Touching the blindfold in my pocket, I took note of Liam's face, evaluated it. It was ovoid, which one might take for granted, though not uncommon are round, seemingly square, cuboid, pear-shaped, globular, asymmetrical, or even rhomboidal heads and faces. Liam's face was familiar enough that I didn't really see it anymore. The face was what many would call "kind," I supposed. The kindness came from eyes and teeth, the latter of which were isolated in their presentation, i.e. he had minor gaps. Despite much effort, I couldn't pin down what I actually knew about him, his history, his loves.

I considered our robotic driver. It might as well have been a self-driving car—the miles driven, turns taken, acceleration, braking, and conversations generated within it: all catalogued for the greater efficiency of the system. Not only would the car's cameras record you, but also your heartbeat, breaths, thoughts, feelings, dreams. Across from each other, Liam and I discussed the luxury of the black SUV, the smooth ride, the lavish interior, the wonder of the mirrored ceiling. We looked out the tinted windows behind one another's respective faces.

Liam asked when he would hear the whole story, meaning, I assumed, the story behind our stretch SUV ride, and who had provided it. But what if he was hinting at something else? I told him there was no such thing as a whole story. Only fragments.

When pressed, I said my employer had received a large grant from the Supranational Association of Information Destruction (SAID) and that the leftover funds had to be used somehow. I asked Liam if he had ever paid for the company of a woman.

"Of course," he said.

This initiated a chronicle of Liam's experiences in the *Rossebuurt* of Amsterdam, in Las Vegas, in Thailand, on Hamburg's *Reeperbahn*, and so on. I speculated as to how much of what he said was fiction, how much he knew, and whether he was pleased with the network of near-truths I was fashioning.

Industrial structures passed outside, tinted by darkened window film and the falling evening light. The buildings aged as the vehicle pushed west. Factories, train yards, and massive warehouses rose around us. We could have been approaching water, shipyards, the meatpacking district. A smell of something unlike any of those things rose and trailed after the car. Asparagus growing in fecal matter.

20

We halted in a nearly empty parking lot in front of a seafood restaurant-cum-marina that abutted a foul, slow-moving harbor steeped in the byproducts of heavy industry. Though I knew this wasn't the case, the restaurant and parking lot had the feel of an elaborate movie set. The driver exited and opened the door to my right, exposing Liam and I to the fading light as we both downed drinks. Standing outside felt odd, unsteady— we had consumed a significant portion of the mezcal. I thought about the worm, and what it would be like to grow inside and feed on another living being. Perhaps it wouldn't be entirely foreign. The driver, I realized outside of the vehicle, was incredibly tall, as in 15-25 inches taller than myself, and (important to note) 19-29 inches taller than Liam. I handed the driver the envelope Blanche had given me.

The driver withdrew, bending in half, then in half again, then in half again, until he disappeared into the vehicle, which kept running as we approached the restaurant. The building was a multi-story wooden affair that violated at least one fire code. It was bordered on one side by rows of slips extending out into the harbor, and on the other by a disused fish processing plant. We crunched through dusty gravel to the main entrance, whose doors parted to reveal a young man.

"Welcome to the Weeping Willow," he said.

"Not a very nautical name, is it," Liam said.

The young man was wearing a tight black silk vest

over a white dress shirt and skinny white silk tie. White slacks; no apparent underwear. He asked us to follow him through the lobby, lined by photos of movie stars who had dined in the building over its many years. The young man said that every other President of the United States had eaten in their establishment, though he declined to answer, or was merely silent when I asked if the current president had visited. He left us with the hostess, a young woman in a dark blue pencil dress covered in anchors who resembled the doorman in nearly every physical way.

"Welcome, gentlemen." The hostess stated her name, or a name, and asked if we would be dining, or perhaps enjoying drinks? The quality of seduction she emanated into the air we breathed was professional, even weapons-grade, in its power.

Liam said we'd be dining, at least—emphasis on the "at least." Perhaps I should've monitored his intake in the SUV.

"We have a reservation," I said.

"[Unintelligible]," Liam said.

"Yes, I have you right here," she said. "Follow me, please."

The hostess preceded us the way a woman does when unaware or pretending to be unaware that someone following is observing every movement her body makes through space. We followed her down hallways and up stairs, Liam in particular making no effort to unglue his gaze from the flexion and extension of arms, legs, hips, and shoulders, the abduction and adduction of the legs from the hips, the elevation and depression of, well, you know. She led us to a private banquet room, a rectangle, one side of which was a jalousie-windowed view of the shitty harbor. The hostess hit a switch on the wall, opening the jalousie windows or louvre windows or louver-windows in unison.

The hostess urged us to seat ourselves at a black table-clothed table, intimately lit. We sat with our backs to the window view of the pungent, roiling harbor. She lit candles, placed stationary pads and golf pencils at each of our places. We were told to write down up to three names, and that should we write more than three, management would exercise discretion in choosing among our selections. With this, she seemed to glide backwards out of the room, doors closing silently in her wake.

A woman entered wearing a navy blue cap-sleeve babydoll dress and carrying a bottle of 1989 Branaire Ducru, which she uncorked for us. A woman entered who resembled my childhood friend's babysitter, the one who teased in so many ways. She was wearing the same outfit I always pictured, and carrying two steaming tureens of cream of roasted walnut soup. A woman named Ernestine entered. A woman entered who resembled Blanche in every visible respect. Her name was Whitney.

A woman in a kimono entered, carrying two arugula, fennel, apricot, rocquefort, pecan, and ginger steak salads. A woman entered who resembled my high school's head cheerleader in nearly every respect, except she wasn't blonde. A woman entered who resembled my youngest sister. Liam began chatting with her. He asked her a question that in many circumstances would be considered distasteful.

"That's one of the few things I can't do," she said, smiling intensely.

A woman entered carrying two platters of pan seared salmon with avocado remoulade. A woman in a life-jacket entered with a bottle of 1996 Ducru Beaucaillou. A woman named Petra sauntered in, wearing a form-fitting heather grey off-the-shoulder dress with what I believe is called "ruching." Two women dressed in ill-fitting Boy Scout uniforms entered the room, offering strawberries in outstretched hands. Liam began to fade from my awareness.

During a pause in the festivities, we took turns visiting the bathroom, Liam handing off powder wrapped in plastic to me under the table. The hostess returned in pink garb, wearing what is called a "peplum" or an article of clothing to which a "peplum" is attached. Her earrings were tiny swaying anchors. She urged us to not forget our stationary pads, and added that should we need assistance—liquid, gustatory, medical, chemical, or otherwise—that we not hesitate to pick up the red phone in the next room. The first name I scribbled was Whitney's, the one who resembled Blanche in nearly every respect. Something struck me about the names: Blanche and Whitney? I engaged in what might be considered "cheating" by writing the names of both women wearing Boy Scout uniforms under #2, followed by a third name.

21

Whitney, Blanche's spitting-image, stepped into my room in a serape, a sarong, a sari, or whatever it was you called it. I noticed minor scars, a lack of tan lines, the ghost of a rib cage. Whitney resembled a movie star from the silent film era, a halo playing around her edges. The urges I experienced, in order: the urge to view, the problematic urge to save, the urge to interview, the euphemistic urge to woo.

As I said, she looked like Blanche. Whitney's voice, as far as I could tell, was smokier. When she spoke, she dragged out the last syllable of certain words to the point of near-discomfort. Her lower body was emphasized by the item that connects a woman's stockings to her underwear. Everything was red, including the walls and telephone. She said that for the price I paid, even kissing was allowed. I said I had some questions first.

Age: Young enough to lend the number an aphrodisiacal quality, old enough to prevent a sense of guilt

Siblings: None

Country of origin: United States

State of origin: This one

Community of origin: A suburb populated by the upper-middle class

Parents: Stable, loving, supportive

Highest level of education: Partially completed Master of Arts in Gender Studies

Other degrees: Bachelor of Arts in film

High school: One of the two prep schools that people may have heard of

Political leanings: Obvious

Reasons for entering the profession: To make significant cash in a time-efficient manner, to slake an in-her-opinion more-powerful-than-normal sex drive, to help people

"Help people?" I asked.

"Not you. Other people," she said.

Whitney pushed me onto a Tempurpedic Tempur-Cloud Supreme Mattress, complete with armature of red silk bedding set. She asked if I was worried she had looming student loans, if I thought she needed therapy, if I thought she was a tourist too. I could feel an episode of the spins coming on. Episode as in part of a television series.

"All the girls here are free range," she said, straddling me.

"What do you know about Donovan Foley?" I asked.

"Since you're on track to becoming my customer of the month, I'll tell you."

Favorite drugs: cannabis (plus prescription amphetamine for lethargy plus alcohol for the jitters), cocaine (plus Alprazolam for the sleeplessness, irritability, and anxiety), ecstasy plus acid aka "candy-flipping," ketamine.

"I know he comes here," she said. "But don't worry—he's never been a client of mine."

"Who does he see?" I asked, still on my back.

She whispered the name I had written down as #3. Her hair was in my face as she started to take my clothes off.

"You look just like someone I know," I said. I tried to will my hands to move.

"That's why they put me here, sugarplum."

The women whose names I had written down next to #2 entered the red room dressed in ill-fitting Boy Scout uniforms. If the allure of Blanche's double was clear, the logic of the approaching fantasy was somehow linked to my childhood. Not to the Scouting organization per se—I was ejected as a Tenderfoot for using a bulldozer to tip over a port-a-potty containing Scoutmaster Hellström—but to something far more formative. In April of 2001, a time of alleged bygone innocence for the country and myself, Destiny's Child appeared on Saturday morning television at the Nickelodeon Kids' Choice Awards. The trio were dressed, inexplicably, in altered Boy Scout uniforms: forest-green shorts or pants, long-sleeve khaki uniform shirt, folded up and under to bare the midriff (in the case of Kelly and Beyoncé) or with two or three of the lowest buttons unbuttoned and the shirt chevroned open and secured in the back (in the case of Michelle). The regulation green web belts with bronze buckles, too, made a lasting impression.

Anyhow, the pair of attendants entered the red room costumed as Destiny's Child costumed as Boy Scouts. When the door was shut behind them, they stood for a moment, taking me in. They both wore the chilly runway look that works its magic without fail. The one who was slightly taller said her name was Reagan. Her partner's name was such that the two names, when paired, formed the name of a famous Hollywood actor. Reagan dragged her tongue over glossy lips in a slow arc.

The first powder they provided for our enjoyment

sharpened something inside me, and dulled something else. My body ceased functioning in the way I was accustomed. Reagan switched on speakers in the room's corner, filling the air with what may have been a brown note. The two of them flanked a lamp, and sort of shimmied there, watching me. I was reminded of Giotto's *Death and Ascension of St. Francis*, for the angels of course but also for what was hidden inside the cloud. In foreground: corpse, mourners, roughly ten haloed angels (some with illegible faces), and the ascendant St. Francis. The cloud, though, contained the face of what could only be a devil, demon, imp, daemon, fiend, or fallen angel. What else watches from a cloud?

The better question: what did "demon" really mean? Blanche, I was sure, rejected the label, and perhaps had ties to some falling under this designation. The only things of interest to Blanche, it seemed, shined with enough intensity to make direct viewing of the source impossible. Whatever power her associates had, it emanated from an ability to control brightness, to blur certain aspects of themselves, or, in effect, to cloud a mind or two. Foley, for example.

The second powder they gave me caused my body to sink into what felt like a jelly-filled bag. A series of sounds: paper being shredded in slow-motion, a chainsaw backwards, the sound of a single finger snap echoing, extended until it sounded like a hiss of flame. I breathed heavy electricity. A layer of clear glass emerged between my eyes and surroundings, which then shattered, reemerged, and shattered, until the ceiling extended into an infinite corridor. Woodland paths and streams became visible in the tile, a maze buzzed into the hair on someone's gargantuan head. The pair of attendants were sitting on the edge of the bed, talking.

"They always say they can go forever," Reagan said.

"Like, I'm going to fuck you for hours," the other said.

"Then, a few minutes later…"

They were laughing. The room grew smaller as pieces of my body elongated, siphoned off into a zone of immense pressure. I became convinced the two of them were planning to kidnap, torture, and kill me. I could hear them discussing this while I was paralyzed. I heard one whisper the phrase "make him disappear for good." Their plan, as I heard it, was to render me unconscious with an electroshock weapon, tie me up, and load me into the trunk of a little gray Honda: a Civic or an Accord. They wouldn't stop on the way to the countryside. They would weight the handcuffs and legcuffs binding me so that I'd be unable to generate noise by striking the trunk's roof. Their plan was to drive to a secluded rural area, forested, park the car, and tie me to a tree. The final component of this plan, of which I grew more certain with each passing second (though each passing second, due to time dilation, felt stretched to at least a minute and a half), was to take out my gag and torture me to death while filming the process.

Most purported snuff films are not only hoaxes, but highly unoriginal. In fact, none have been verified, if one considers the definition of "snuff" as a commercially sold film containing an actual murder. Though tapes have been seized as evidence in murder cases, none of them, so far, have featured the actual moment of death.

More importantly, the murders themselves were not undertaken for the purpose of commercial entertainment. Numerous films contain footage of dead bodies, though never the final moment. More than one entirely fake film, from the 1970s in particular, has been crafted in such a painstakingly elaborate and realistic fashion as to incite a panic. Accidental deaths don't count. Wartime footage doesn't count. According to my research, however, Charles Manson and his Family did perhaps record a snuff film in 1969 using equipment stolen from an NBC-TV truck. More concretely, signs point to a snuff film of Al Goldstein's last moments, authorized by the pornography and free speech agitator himself.

Even more concretely, according to what I was about to learn, one of the biggest snuff games in snuff town, the Coca-Cola Company of Snuff, the Francis Ford Coppola of Snuff, the Ringling Brothers Barnum and Bailey Circus of Snuff, The Oscar Mayer of Snuff, The Vladimir Putin of Snuff, The Steven Spielberg of Snuff, The Cirque du Soleil of Snuff, the Queen Mother of Snuff, the Maersk Triple E Class Container Ship of Snuff, the Stay-Puft Marshmallow Man of Snuff, the Queen Mary 2 Ocean Liner of Snuff, the Cthulhu of Snuff, the Warren Buffett of Snuff, the Son of Sam of Snuff, the Big Black Monolith of Snuff, the King Ghidorah of Snuff, the Rasputin of Snuff, the Godzilla of Snuff, the Issei Sagawa of Snuff, the Mount McKinley of Snuff, the Superorganism of Snuff, the Great Barrier Reef of Snuff, the African Bush Elephant of Snuff, the Sauropod of Snuff, the Saltwater Crocodile of Snuff, the Blue Whale of Snuff, the White Whale of Snuff, the Cleopatra VII Philopator of Snuff, the Holy Ghost of Snuff, the Emperor of Snuff, the Godfather of Snuff, the Man Behind the Curtain of Snuff, the Caesarion of Snuff, the Taipei 101 of Snuff, the Sultan of Snuff himself, was none other than Lucian Bevacqua.

22

I was alone in the red room's bed, sudoriferous glands pumping, sweat cool on my half naked body. When a woman named Ernestine entered the room, I was no longer convinced that the previous pair had intended to torture and murder me, though my vision remained somewhat distorted, coming down. She was wearing three articles of clothing: a sheath dress and two shoes, all identically iridescent. I stood up and found my pants. The sound system kicked on: pure static, followed by metallic lounge sound. I felt like I was circling the drain.

"I need to ask you about Donovan Foley." I said.

"I thought you looked like the inquisitive type," Ernestine said.

She claimed to invoke physician-patient confidentiality, then attorney-client privilege. I asked who was who in these relationships. She sat down on a red leather chesterfield sofa, motioning for me to join her. The leather was cold. She removed her pumps, revealing a shimmering hue of toenail polish matching dress, shoes, and maybe even eyes (I couldn't look at them, or into them, for some time).

"He's the client, I'm patient," she said.

"Can you describe him?" I asked.

I told her I could give her information in return.

"Everyone says they have information, and wants more of it. My job has nothing to do with information."

"What do you see when you look at his face? If it's anything like what I've seen, I need to know."

The sense of play in Ernestine's tone changed into

something else. It occurred to me that the intimate video footage I had seen of Liam and Blanche could actually have been Liam and Whitney. Meaning: that Blanche hadn't been hiding a relationship from me, but had been hiding Liam's link to Vector, and that Vector, in some capacity, had sent Liam to the Weeping Willow before.

"Donovan's face is all hole," she said. "But it isn't like that all the time."

"What causes it?"

"It doesn't matter," she said.

"So he comes to see you?"

"I'm the only one he sees."

I asked her what Donovan Foley's desires were, what he usually did with her. She said she would oblige me.

"I'll tell you because it sounds so mundane," she said. "Whenever Donovan visits me, he makes small talk while he paces. He takes off his coat and asks me to close my eyes. He covers my eyes with a blindfold, leaves them covered for varying periods of time. He always pays for two hours, but rarely stays that long."

"What does he do to you while you are blindfolded?"

"The funny thing is: I don't know."

"He doesn't touch you?"

"No. He's silent, staring at me or at the floor, for all I know. Maybe he's inches from my face. There is a sensation though."

"What kind of sensation?"

"Sometimes all it takes is fifteen minutes. The feeling is like being mentally frisked. Like I'm a filing cabinet he's rifling through."

"What do you know about his personal life?"

"You're moving in the wrong direction," she said. "Vector doesn't care about Donovan Foley—they only want Bevacqua."

"Why?"

"Because of the films. If you look deeper into his catalogue you'll find terrible things."

"Such as?"

"Snuff. Actual snuff, as well as simulated. He's the biggest director of the stuff in North America, and what he hasn't directed he has produced."

"Why hasn't he been arrested?"

"The films are so underground they barely exist. Who would arrest him?"

"The police? The FBI? INTERPOL?"

"Let's be clear. Bevacqua doesn't deal with children—even he has limits. Or different preferences, at least."

"Why should I believe any of this?"

"Believe what you want, but ask yourself: why would Bevacqua be arrested by the main consumers of his product?"

"I don't follow."

"When is a snuff tape not a snuff tape?"

I said nothing.

"When it's evidence."

Logic pointed to the likelihood that someone—Blanche, Ernestine, Fister, Liam—was lying. Perhaps I was lying. Perhaps everyone was lying, or deluded, to varying degrees. Ernestine appeared sane, convinced, and unconcerned with my belief in her assertion that one man supplied most of the U.S. (if not the continent) with snuff films in order to secure convictions. Bevacqua's snuff, she said, was caviar to the general.

"Let me leave with you," Ernestine said.

She claimed that when we were finished, her night was over. Ten minutes later—or 20 or 25 or 30 or 45—we exited the red room and passed through a series of hallways to an elevator. Ernestine had wrapped herself in a trench coat. I fingered the blindfold in my suit coat pocket, picturing scenarios that would call for its use, picturing Foley dead on a slab or trussed up on a conveyor belt, moving towards heat in an aggressive food processing environment. The elevator released us into a warm stairwell containing a metal door leading to the outside. Opening it, I had the impression it was a door whose exterior matched the painted brick around it and whose outline would disappear upon closing. The belt of Ernestine's trench coat trailed after her, manipulated by wind, as she clattered toward the parked SUV. Its engine turned over in the nearly empty lot. I hurried after her, wishing she was dragging me by the hand, hoping for another moment of contact before entering the car.

Inside, an examination of the mezcal bottle revealed no sign of the worm. The most I could hope for was that each item I ingested at Vector's behest would lead to a form of progress, a minor step forward. The SUV began moving through the industrial landscape, hard lines and intersecting fields of tan, gray, umber, rust, and the occasional citrine.

"What do you plan to do when you come face to face?" Ernestine asked.

I pictured a figure emerging from mist.

"I have to give him something."

"What would that be?" she asked, reclining against the leather interior.

"A sealed letter. From Vector."

"Do you know what's inside?"

I replied that I did not. Ernestine proceeded, in a way that was perhaps unsurprising, to further complicate matters. She warned me against the following actions:

1. *Opening the letter at once*

2. *Destroying the letter at once*

3. *Delivering the letter to its intended target*

The vehicle rolled on, leaving seafood and Liam in the distance. Maybe he was in the trunk of a Honda. As we rolled, visions of the interstate highway system loomed in my imagination: all the loops, all the connections, all the horrible things taking place on the highways, next to them, and at every exit. All the traffic, the profit, and people who would kill to protect it. I considered, not for the first time, giving up the entire enterprise. Bevacqua was clearly dangerous—whether or not on a near-mythical level was up to conjecture. Was Ernestine to be believed? Was Bevacqua the main source of recorded violence in this hemisphere? Surely not. Were it true, such a revelation would be on the order of the revelation that someone was always watching. Was it such a leap from observation to violence? Faced with that kind of power, my options were to make myself invisible to it or to attract its notice. I feared I had already done the latter, and had trouble explaining my need to be noticed in this way. Maybe I wanted what Foley had: his glamour, his form of camouflage, his connection to Bevacqua. How dangerous could a film director be?

Curiosity, too, was driving me forward. I was nearly curious enough to open the letter to Foley—presuming it was a letter—though this was the first thing Ernestine had warned me against. If I couldn't open it, shouldn't destroy it, and if actually delivering it was a bad idea, what was I to do? As long as I kept the unopened letter, a version of Schrödinger's untested bullet, perhaps I'd be safe.

"Why shouldn't I deliver the letter?" I asked.

"Vector doesn't want to help you," she said.

"And you do?"

"Yes, by convincing you to trust no one, including myself. The most I can say is to think hard about why Vector wants to get you close to Foley."

The SUV paused at a red light, and Ernestine prostrated herself and moved toward me on her hands and knees. I held my breath as she came to rest between my legs, her touch moving over my body. Her hands were in my jacket pockets, and I watched her pull out the blindfold. The second she brought it over her eyes the familiar effect occurred, her face blurred in the manner of Foley's. Someone was now between my legs whose face I couldn't see. Ernestine opened the door and stepped into the street. I watched her walk until the visible parts of her disappeared as well.

23

The next time I fed a piece of paper into a shredder, it hit me. Shredding felt nearly as good as watching a Bevacqua fragment. What I did was mindless, but it accomplished what I was sure the creation of art accomplished: it allowed me to stop thinking. Perhaps this was less ecstatic than the grand visions Bevacqua was making out of the fabric of life, but wasn't document destruction somehow noble in its own way?

Days had passed and I was reabsorbed into the flows and rhythms of work. Instead of working all day and creeping all night, I was shredding all day and streaming all night. My collection of Bevacqua ephemera, marginalia, and juvenilia grew to massive proportions. I bought a respectable analogue watch, one that ticked with a dividing line whose circular path I could follow with joy.

My first task one morning was to shred the contents of several duffel bags that had been mailed to our location. This job was easier than most in that it required no end-to-end security, meaning I wasn't forced to drive a truck to the origin of the documents, load the documents into our secure truck, return with the documents, and lock them in our storage area before shredding them within a 24-hour period. The sender of the duffel bags happened to be a hospital, which wasn't unusual.

I turned on the 650-Sheet Cross-Cut Shredder/Baler Combo and waited for it to warm up. I opened a duffel bag and pulled out one of the document boxes inside, using a box cutter on the box and turning it upside down. The process was repeated until I had six stacks of paper roughly two feet high. There were roughly 36,000 pages present, though this estimate assumed the pages were of equal thickness.

I had destroyed hard drives, disk drives, and other media. I had destroyed microfiche in an incinerator that reached 2000 degrees Fahrenheit. Feeding medical records into the throat of the shredder, I considered inserting Vector's letter to Foley, which I had been keeping on my person during waking hours, and locked away while I slept. The way the shredder worked, you didn't have to shove—all you had to do was release paper into its slanted mouth. The documents crackled as they moved into the device, making a sound like fire before touching the blades. Shredding the letter was out of the question— it would be akin to Russian roulette. The attraction of waiting was that I could always destroy it later, unless it was opened, that is, or unless something prevented its destruction.

I spent most of my hours (working, waking, and otherwise) thinking about Foley and his connection to Bevacqua. If Fister was to be believed—and who could really say—then Foley had already tried to scare me off his trail. Were Foley and Bevacqua friends, lovers, pals, confidantes? Were they related? Did they share patient-doctor privilege? Lawyer-client privilege? Had they shared needles? Drinks—i.e. after one had taken a drink did the other sip from the same cup, glass, flagon, stein, flask? If one had a communicable disease was it likely the other shared this predicament? Was one the employee of the other, or were they business partners? Was one the angel investor, so to speak? Were they involved in a master-slave dialectic? Who had issued the order to push the man in the brown suit over the edge—Foley or Bevacqua? Did they accomplish this through post-hypnotic suggestion, threats regarding his family, or did one of them somehow "walk into" his consciousness and make him pull the trigger? A better question: was Bevacqua even aware of me, and did I want him to be aware of me? More than one online personage, or the same person under different names, had warned me to get out while I was still able.

At this point, however, I had agreed to perform a service for Vector, an entity seemingly larger than Bevacqua, larger and more or less more legitimate. Much of what circulated concerning the director struck me as sheer invention. The idea that he could be the sole supplier of snuff films to police departments in need of evidence failed the most elementary principles of logic. If the rumors were fantasy, then how to find the real? I needed to see more footage of Donovan Foley.

I had been to the dark parts of the Internet, and they weren't that dark. OK—some of them were dark, but no darker than what was on the surface. All information concerning Bevacqua I had found on the visible, indexed web, not in the dark of the deep part, though much of this information was contradictory. For example, a website claimed the director was born in an unspecified Eastern Bloc country during the 1950s before moving to the US and becoming involved with organized crime, the source of funding for all his early films. I searched for copies of the early work but found only bootleg versions at exorbitant prices, upwards of several thousand dollars per copy. A few titles:

Basement Without a Door
Nude Fish
Elvis and Erebus
Proto-Indo-European Entropy
Earth's Thirteen Most Scenic Prisons
Senators in Kitchens
Tortoise Heaven
Demons on Long Retractable Leashes
Blonde Python
Ensemble for Unicyclists

I again considered inserting the Vector letter into the shredder. Would this be a kind of absolution, or something closer to self destruction? I thought about the tunnel boring machines (TBMs) in slow motion under many a metropolis, and the supposed Shadow Highway System depicted in Bevacqua's film. The way they cut through solid rock, earth, and sand resembled an active and forward-moving paper shredder of enormous size, rendered tubular and tipped on its side. A single TBM moving at a rate of 35 feet per day would have resulted in an excessive tunneling time, considering the distance between the coasts (with digressions) was roughly 2,500 miles, with each mile consisting of 5,280 feet, totaling 13,200,000 feet. Divided by 35 feet per day, 13,200,000 feet resulted in 377,142.857 days or 1,033.2681 years. With 1,000 TBMs, the excavation would have taken one year, with 500 it would have taken two years, with

250 four years, with 125 eight years, with 62.5 sixteen years, etc. Perhaps Eisenhower had assigned a shadow crew to labor beneath the surface of each highway crew at work on the Dwight D. Eisenhower National System of Interstate and Defense Highways, each TBM thereof weighing 1,000 tons and resembling a metal tube slightly longer than a football field. Rotating blades at the TBM's head would have shredded earth and pulverized rock, material moving through the machine via conveyor belt and deposited behind it like a trail of excrement. Perhaps the accompanying "tunnel gang" was killed at the end of construction, much like the myth surrounding the builders of the pyramids (falsely suggested by Herodotus). I did know that a list of countries containing ancient pyramidal structures was long enough to make one wonder.

One of our hospital clients required a certificate of destruction after the shredding was completed. I printed one, signed as a witness, folded it, and stuck it into a stamped envelope with the rest of the outgoing mail. There were nights when the sound of shredding incorporated itself into my dreams.

I hadn't spoken to Liam since our night out—I assumed he made it home in one piece. Neither had I spoken to Blanche, though she had attempted to reach me several times. She called once each morning around the same time, like a telemarketer, and I didn't answer. I imagined her calling 20 individuals simultaneously with an auto-dialer, myself included. If more than one answered, all but the first to answer would be speaking to a dead line. Blanche was surely under a great deal of pressure to establish contact with Foley and Co. In all likelihood, I wasn't their only route to do so, as much as I wanted to be. Or did I? I couldn't be the only one any more than Liam could or Blanche could or Whitney could. Were the latter two twins, coincidental doubles, or the same person? Had the blindfold that Ernestine wore done something to her face, or something to my vision? I contemplated what one could accomplish with a device like that.

An employee of the US Postal Service arrived with a package requiring my signature. The mail carrier was no-nonsense, on-the-move, eager for me to sign. I wondered if she was truly a USPS employee. She wore the regulation light blue polo shirt under an approved dark blue insulated vest, Postal Regulation Reebok Black Leather Cross-Trainers, and a Letter Carrier Waterproof Sun Helmet. The return address listed was that of Vector Industries. For all I knew, she could've worked for Vector. But why would Vector send one of their own when they could easily send something through the mail? To keep an eye on the object? To assure end-to-end security? To engage in two-for-one delivery plus establishing visual contact with the target?

I gave up my signature, something that, if harvested, I found more invasive than merely being watched. What could be done to a captive, what could be taken: fluids from the body, the body itself, vivisection and study. What could be done to someone from afar: information gathering, a copy of all subject output, what the subject does, what the subject produces, images and video thereof. A signature, a mark, a trail, that which is left behind. The residue in the snail's wake. Inside the package was a note from Blanche that thanked me for my services and expounded on the nature of the enclosed gift.

Inside the package was a laptop, sent in the event that a return to the Vector building might prove too strenuous, sent as a reward for my recent performance. Or, I thought, sent to prevent me drifting away, sent to allow me access to their information and allow them access in turn.

I turned on the gift and waited for it to boot up. Somewhere in the office was a box of USB drives marked "clean." I had purchased the drives with cash from a store small enough to have no cameras, or at least no camera at the register, no visible camera. CDs and other electronic items were often identified with a batch number which could be linked to an electronic transaction. Similarly, you could be followed to a post office drop box, could have your mail grabbed covertly. On each USB drive was a copy of anonymizing software to conceal my location and browsing habits through encryption. I was a small fish. The problem, however, with such encryption, was that though it shielded one from the vast majority of surveillance techniques, its use served as a beacon to those higher on the food chain. Consider a neighborhood at night composed of homes with varying degrees of security. The most secure home in the neighborhood, however, the one with the most advanced alarm system would also be the most visible—illuminated by floodlights of the highest intensity from every direction.

Always assume another layer. Hiding yourself with software signaled to the observant that you had something to hide. After inserting the USB drive, I ran the secure browser it contained and performed an image search.

"Donovan Foley" (many irrelevant results found, all with faces)

"Lucian Bevacqua" (no results found)

"Blanche_______" (familiar fetching photo from Vector office party)

Was I part of a love triangle of sorts, or a multi-dimensional figure with more than three sides, a love network? How was this triangulation of desire operating, and how might it resolve? Perhaps my desire itself was triangular, or tri-horned: desire for Bevacqua, desire for Donovan, desire for Blanche, or desire for knowledge thereof. In each of these cases, my desire was nourished by its lack of fulfillment. Attainment of the desired would puncture the mystery, filling the lack forever. Or would it? To be with Blanche (rather than someone who looked like her), to be in the presence of Bevacqua, to see Foley's face. Perhaps there was a way to accomplish each of these acts simultaneously. To skewer myself on the horns of a tri-lemma.

I used the laptop to log into Vector's surveillance service, typing in Liam's address. His face came into view on my screen, accompanied by the sounds of typing. I reclined in my black office chair, observing Liam reclining in his, watched him on my screen as I entertained the possibility he was watching me on his. Surely not. The odds would be against that kind of serendipity, unless Liam was always watching me on his screen, unless that had been his job all along. If Liam's assignment was to keep an eye on me, odds would favor the possibility that whenever I viewed current footage of Liam, he would at that time be viewing current footage of me. If this were indeed his assignment, I considered when he would sleep, relieve himself, eat. Clearly, he could eat at his desk, or simply bring his laptop to the kitchen, observing during the process of food preparation. As for the other, I surmised as well that Vector's putative surveillance policy might state that the observer was allowed to relieve him- or herself at such time as would coincide with the target's pattern of bodily elimination. Nevertheless, it would be advisable to enact one of two policies, if not a combination of both: 1) instructing the observer engaged in constant surveillance to catch up on any missed footage, preferably each morning, by observing the previous day's bathroom breaks and fast forwarding through the footage of sleep, on a separate screen, while keeping an eye on the target's current activities as well 2) employing two (or even three, or more) observers to observe the target in shifts. How many person-hours are required to observe and log one person's daily existence?

I don't know why I decided to give Liam a call. Perhaps that isn't completely true. If he happened to be watching me, I wanted to show him I had an inkling, to show him that whenever he was staring into me I was in turn staring back into him. I placed tape over the webcam lens embedded at the top of the laptop's screen. The tape was gray, and I planned to keep it there, even if it accomplished nothing. I had the feeling that people with access to webcams had other ways to see me: through the monitor, through the television, through cameraphones, etc. You no longer pick up the phone to make or answer a call— usually you're already holding it. I dialed the number and looked at Liam on the screen; he was leaning back in his black reclining office chair with mesh back and nylon base, hands behind his head, elbows out. When his phone began to ring, I watched Liam lean forward, glance at the ringing object on his desk, and rustle around in a drawer. The video feed was replaced with a pale yellow image. It appeared Liam had affixed a post-it note to his webcam.

I typed the address of Donovan Foley's house, bringing up a map of the neighborhood. The route I had walked from the subway station was amply dotted with red symbols indicating a camera that could be accessed: security cameras outside garages, webcams, cell phones, nanny cams in living rooms, CCTV cameras on streetlamps, unidentified sources of surveillance. I had the sense that my own circuit, the path I was on, was an increasingly tightening closed circuit whose center I couldn't yet comprehend. I found the spot along the way where I had paused to look through a window— the dilapidated storefront filled with dusty objects—and clicked the symbol to view the feed. What appeared was footage of the street from inside the disused shop, its dusty front window framing a view of the sidewalk. Seed pods floated through the air. The angle of view was from the level of the workbench I had seen. I realized I was seeing the street from the point of view of the headless doll. The perception that I was being watched had been correct in the extreme. But watched by whom? Foley, Blanche, Liam, someone else entirely? The urge struck me to visit one of the many storage lockers in our warehouse, empty it completely, spray it with a high-pressure hose, strip naked, set my clothing on fire, enter the storage locker, close the door, lock it, assume the fetal position, and rock myself to sleep.

The house that I had been inside, the one belonging to Foley, the one that resembled a safe house in disuse, had two feeds associated with it on the map. One remained unchanged: the view of a room with red wall, chair, and calendar. The second feed, on which I clicked, featured only the ceiling: clean, white paint, a light fixture with two bulbs: one burning, one burned out, resulting in two half-circles of light and shadow. The sound of a blender accompanied this image. I closed the program.

24

The entrance to Erebus was an unmarked door in a back alley. Above the door was a red light protected by a wire cage—the bulb had likely been broken previously, by a bottle or something else. I pushed the door open and on the other side a bouncer asked for my ID. The lighting was red inside as well. I climbed stairs to the first of several crowded rooms. Nearly everyone was wearing black: t-shirts bearing Gothic script, leather, silk, costumes constructed of feathers and rayon, their wearers resembling dark angels, fairies, butterflies. I ordered a drink at the long bar, and scanned the crowd for Blanche. On the wall was a quote attributed to Hesiod:

In truth at first Chaos came to be, but next wide-bosomed Earth, the ever-sure foundation of all the deathless ones who hold the peaks of snowy Olympus, and dim Tartarus in the depth of the wide-pathed Earth, and Eros, fairest among the deathless gods, who unnerves the limbs and overcomes the mind and wise counsels of all gods and all men within them. From Chaos came forth Erebus and black Night...

Foley had made a film called *Elvis and Erebus*, though copies were prohibitively expensive. What could its content be? Anything, potentially. Elvis clearly didn't star, but maybe an impersonator. Maybe it was the story of the King's pact with Satan, exchanging his immortal soul for earthly success and the ability to live on in the bodies of Vegas-bound performers, seriatim, until the end of this century. A sort of living dead arrangement. I drifted through the club, the occasional burly biker-type, waif, and manic pixie sleepwalker giving me the odd look—perhaps my plain black T wasn't enough to blend in. I needed piercings, more visible tattoos, leather, maybe even a little letter. Each room featured different music, all of it hard and fast.

Either Blanche located me or I located her or we located each other in one of many red-lit rooms. Her clothing was monochromatically apropos: boots, tights, skirt, leather jacket. It occurred to me that an obvious anagram of "Elvis" is "evils." Likewise "evilness" and "vileness" were minor variations on some larger theme. The title of the film itself could be rearranged to form:

enviable duress
abused sniveler
bad seer unveils
evil seabed urns
sad unbelievers
enabled viruses
blade universes
bad ensures evil
devil rune bases
bad urine vessel

"I've always wanted to meet a Satanist," I said.

"They really run the gamut," Blanche said.

She pointed out several specimens. For the first one, a youngish man, she claimed Satanism was merely a form of role-play, of theatrics. Another one supposedly became involved for the symbols alone. Another got into it for shock value. Yet another prayed to the Dark One the way anyone prayed to anyone. This one didn't believe in deities, thought of Satan as a construct, an ideal, a goal for individual self-realization. That one, she said, was probably actually evil. This one believed only in the body. That one called herself a Pagan, this one a practitioner of Gnosticism, that one a follower of obscure Greco-Roman mystery religions. That one believed in what he understood as a Demiurge, a deity linked to the material world. This one, she claimed, pointing, had a mind that was closed to her.

Blanche led me to a cordoned off area blocked by two large men standing in front of massive carmine curtains. She leaned close to one of the men (wearing black suit and black tie), and spoke into his ear. One of them lifted the black ornamental cord, and the other held the curtain aside. We entered a room of dampened sound, even dimmer lights, a small gathering of revelers, a bar, and a low stage.

The room was either larger than it looked, or looked larger than it was. The edges of the room were dark, implying in places that the space continued unseen beyond whatever borders that could be found. Here and there was ambient light—volcanic, but far darker. Tables with candles were sprinkled throughout. Blanche pointed to a couple at one such table. She said the man was Grayson Blanco, out on the town with his wife Lucinda. Lucinda Blanco: it was a bit too much, even for me.

"Be careful around the Blancos," Blanche said. "It's possible one or both of them will try to get you alone."

"What would their motivation be?"

"The usual," she said.

I considered abandoning this and all other projects. Fear, somehow, had bloomed in proportion to my curiosity. The fear was such that description of what I feared was impossible, because to articulate it would only increase the fear. The eeriest dreams are ones involving human faces. Fear might be the oldest emotion, rooted in self-preservation, clearly, rooted in the flight-response. Some frightful dreams that I had had might more accurately be called visions: faraway obscured faces that slowly came closer to reveal a rictus, waking up to a similar rictus directly in front of your face, or the impression that someone else's body, some Other, was in the room with you, or, lastly, a slow-moving visage that performed a lunge or other startling motion. I was growing uncertain of coming face to face with Donovan Foley, while simultaneously realizing that there might be no way around it.

For some reason, we approached the Blancos. Grayson Blanco extended his hand to Blanche, while Lucinda fixed her with a curious look. Grayson Blanco grasped Blanche's hand, bent to kiss it, and offered to shake mine. He said his full name as we shook.

"A bit theatrical, isn't it?" Lucinda asked.

"What's a bit theatrical?" I asked.

"This place. We're longtime friends of the owner. Perhaps you'd like a tour?"

"Maybe later," I said.

"Grayson, this gentleman wants a tour," she said.

"It's quite all right," I said. "Some other time."

"A grappa, then." Lucinda Blanco snapped her fingers, the echo, for acoustic reasons unknown, extending, elongating into a familiar hiss. A slim, shirtless, muscular man in skintight leather pants appeared.

"Four grappas, please," Lucinda Blanco said, and the man disappeared.

"What is it you do?" Grayson Blanco asked. "We know this one's story," he said, pointing to Blanche.

"He's a bit of a film buff," Blanche said.

Grayson Blanco fixed me with a look. "How wonderful," he said.

"What about the two of you?" I asked.

"I'm a lowly programmer," Grayson Blanco said.

"He's a lowly one, all right," Lucinda said.

"And yourself?" I asked her.

"I used to program for a financial services company, now I do the same for a very different kind of company."

Drinks appeared, and we began to sip. It came to my attention that a show was about to start. Lucinda Blanco said the performance was one that you could only see three times before becoming forever changed.

A man and woman appeared onstage, twins in nearly every visible aspect. "Twinning," by the way, holds a twin meaning within itself, and can refer to the action of separating or severing, as in "split in twain," but can also mean to join or unite in association or agreement. The pair seemed to fade-in—I never saw a curtain move, never saw a curtain. The stage, like much of the room, had no perceivable back, and merely continued into black space. The pair were wearing black tights and nothing else. Their exposed skin was oiled. Both were spare, wiry, the woman's chest only slightly distinguishable from the man's. They sported short hair of identical length, in fact likely had identical haircuts: buzzed with clippers on the side, gelled on top, hair peaked impishly. Even eyebrows may have matched, and they were madeup in the same fashion. Aside from that atop heads, no further hair or stubble was apparent anywhere. We moved to the stage, and the crowd closed around us.

What followed was a dance, or what some would call dancing. The figures bounded, floated, ran, leapt balletically, and traced repeating patterns in the manner of screensaver images. Eventually the woman began to rotate, followed by the man repeating the movement. The man in turn revolved in place, after which the woman repeated his movement exactly. The woman struck a pose; the man repeated the pose. The man struck a pose; the woman repeated the pose. Their movements delineated the invisible borders of the stage. Vaguely familiar operatic fragments were piped into the room via unseen speakers:

If you want to know who we are...

Young man, despair...

On many a vase and jar...

On many a screen and fan...

A thing of shreds and patches...

The dancers were no longer visible on the stage. It would be accurate to say they disappeared, fading out as they faded in, but disappearance implies a verifiable act. They were simply gone, as if a heavy black curtain had been silently dropped between performers and observers. As the audience began to clap, Grayson whispered in my ear: "Quickly, follow me." I failed to locate Blanche or

Lucinda Blanco, and watched Grayson elbow through the crowd with a sense of urgency. I felt hands trail over me as I followed. The sensation was one of awakening mosh pit, and the bodies around us seemed to be turning to observe my movement. Grins were suddenly everywhere. I briefly felt a hand between my legs. I pursued Grayson to the bar, jerking away from someone who had gripped my shoulder. He edged behind the bar, pulled me after him through what looked like a steel door, slammed the door, and slid a bolt. We caught our breath in the dim corridor for several moments. The warm, yeasty crowd smell of bacteria metabolizing sweat had followed us through the door.

"What's happening out there?" I asked.

"Each performance is followed by another performance. One in which the audience participates."

When I asked after our companions' wellbeing in the crowd, he said both could look after themselves. Grayson Blanco referred to Blanche as a lure, a plant, a honeypot, said he would explain what he could. We made our way through the corridor to another corridor leading to a small room he said was backstage, adjacent to an exit and dressing rooms. When I asked how he knew about the corridor, he said he and Lucinda were acquaintances of the owner.

"You used the phrase 'longtime friends,' I believe." I said.

"The owner doesn't have friends," he said.

I asked about the snatches of song, where I may have heard them before. Blanco said they were from *The Mikado*, a favorite comic opera of the owner's for the sole reason that it was referenced in a series of letters by a famous repeat killer and serial letter writer, whose letters included inexplicable symbols and the occasional cipher. He quoted from one of the letters:

"But the task of filling up the blanks I rather leave up to you."

A cipher, of course, can refer to the zero-point on a thermometer, a zero in general, a person who serves as a placeholder, a nonentity, a hieroglyph or symbolic character in the broader sense, and a secret manner of writing using cryptograms. To make the obvious connection, Donovan Foley was a cipher in nearly every sense. He and those connected to him were accompanied by a script I had yet to decode. His face was inscrutable, a blank of sorts. I recalled a line of Tennyson's that referred to the sun's "red and cipher face of rounded foolishness."

"I'm not a bad guy," Blanco said. "I only did what Vector demanded. They made me use my technical skills to get to Foley."

"I was told you spied on women through their webcams. That you got off on it, calling them your 'slaves.'"

"Not even a half-truth," he said.

The word "cipher" can be traced to Arabic *cifr*, meaning nought or void, originally a translation of a Sanskrit word for "empty."

"Which half?" I asked.

"Vector is just like any other company, only more so. It's full of competing factions trying to undermine others and strengthen their own position. I refused to perform a service for one of those factions, so they fabricated blackmail evidence to bring me in line."

He went on to suggest Bevacqua was a major shareholder in Vector. An activist shareholder who continually put pressure on management, likely to the displeasure of some elements therein. Foley, again, was the link—an agent or representative of both, which amounted to a conflict of interest.

"Who owns this club?" I asked.

"Hazard a guess," he said.

"Bevacqua."

"Indeed. Despite whatever can be said about the director, he remains a human being. Vector is a corporation, with all the concomitants. Vector isn't faceless, soulless, whatever the cliché may be, but rather many-souled, many-faced. Perhaps faceless because of its many faces. There is a dispersal of responsibility, of identity, a ruthlessness somehow beyond human."

The Blancos, it seemed, had (at least tangentially) aligned themselves with Bevacqua vis-à-vis Vector. A struggle between the director and the corporation was underway, centered on Donovan Foley. According to Grayson, Vector wanted to buy out Bevacqua. His position was too large, however, though short of a controlling stake.

My life, since the airport encounter, had been a series of loops accelerated with each rotation. I was moving so quickly that faces, identities, motives, and values had begun to blur. What did Liam, Blanche, Whitney, Vector, Bevacqua want? I felt as though the answer was directly in front of me, if only I were to change the angle of my vision somehow. Circling the drain wasn't exactly right. It was more of a wax on, wax off: information gained, information lost, something written, something erased, paint applied, paint covered, scene filmed, scene cut, wash, rinse, repeat, repeat.

Grayson urged me toward the exit, saying there was little time to waste, that I shouldn't mention our discussion to anyone at Vector, shouldn't mention his or Lucinda's names to anyone (except perhaps to a certain filmmaker, should I ever make his acquaintance).

"Another question," I said.

"There's always one more," he said.

"What's Bevacqua's Interstate fixation about?"

"That's easy," he said. "The same reason the FBI is interested in the Interstate. It's all online. No need to FOIA anything."

Blanco depressed the push bar on the door marked EXIT, revealing brick stairs leading to the surface. I exited Erebus, hearing yet another steel door close behind me.

25

The following day, while taking a break from my duties as a Document Destruction Technician, I discovered the meaning of Blanco's FBI comment. The Bureau was interested in the Interstate because the Interstate and its environs was littered with bodies. At some point last century, it became clear that a large percentage of the victims of serial killers were picked up on or near America's highways, and that their bodies were likewise often dumped nearby: on the shoulder, in or near rest areas, service stations, truck stops, abandoned structures, fields, forests, badlands, deserts, ridges, gorges, gulches, ravines, parks, valleys, rivers, ponds, channels, streams, basins, lakes, swamps, ditches, and so on. According to the FBI, they find an average of one body per week—usually the body of a woman, usually transient, usually involved in prostitution and/or substance abuse, and usually the woman's disappearance goes unnoticed.

Once a pattern had suggested itself, the FBI employed one of its many databases, to wit: the Violent Criminal Apprehension Program (ViCAP), itself part of a repository called the National Center for the Analysis of Violent Crime, which in turn gave rise to the Highway Serial Killings Initiative. Over 500 murder victims were identified, mostly fitting demographics outlined above, though also including stranded motorists, hitchhikers, and runaways. Hundreds of suspects were also identified, mostly long-haul truckers. A map overlaid with red dots signifying the site where a body has been discovered on or near an Interstate highway suggested one could not drive for an hour, on average, before passing a murder scene. Around America's more populous eastern seaboard, this figure would be closer to 15 minutes. It appeared South Dakota was the only state where no bodies had surfaced, as of yet.

Dozens of former truckers have been imprisoned in America for multiple murders. They've been incriminated via several means: credit card receipts, GPSes affixed by their trucking companies, records of tolls paid by E-ZPass, FasTrak, and other electronic toll collection (ETC) systems, including SunPass, TxTAG, Peach Pass, Good To Go!, K-Tag, MnPass, Palmetto Pass, Pikepass, and GeauxPass. Of course, the single most potent technology used in the apprehension of these mobile killers has been surveillance footage, and the ability to remotely access and search this increasingly high resolution footage with growing computer power.

Joint statement from the American Trucking Associations (ATA) and the Owner-Operator Independent Drivers Association (OOIDA):

Highways are the lifeblood of America, and truckers, if you will, are a key part of the respiratory system that carries oxygen (cargo) to America's bloodstream. Nearly all American truckers are certifiably decent, hardworking individuals in love with the open road and the American Dream. Though a twisted few are indeed dangerous, they do not represent the views of truckers in general, and are a miniscule portion of our overall industry. At last count, there were over 3.5 million men and women employed as professional truck drivers

I discovered online that it was fairly easy to find the location and travel history of any vehicle nationwide, provided you knew the license plate. Not just the FBI, but repo men, hackers, and private individuals of all stripes could do this. Indeed, the license plate database has its corollaries in the FBI's Next Generation Identification (NGI) system (which replaced the Integrated Automated Fingerprint Identification System (IAFIS)), including new functionality in the form of the Interstate Photo System (IPS), a searchable national face recognition service. To state the obvious, every photo of a face on the Internet, including and especially those on social media, is available to law enforcement (and by extension, certain savvy members of the public). I also learned of a searchable photo database consisting of the "scars, marks, tattoos, and symbols" on the bodies of U.S. citizens.

Aside from Interstate 40, the highway mentioned by name in *Pupfish*, there are two other truly coast-to-coast routes: Interstate 10 and Interstate 80. I added 40, 10, and 80, perhaps absurdly, arrived at 130, which I divided by 10. I spent hours looking at a map of the Interstate Highway System stippled with red dots.

When the office phone began to ring, I had an inkling it was time. Or perhaps this is merely my thinking in retrospect, attributing weight to the sound of a call like any other. The number on the electric blue or possibly celeste blue display of the expensive cordless VTech was one I didn't recognize. The area from which the call was made, normally revealed, was designated "Unknown." I added up the digits before answering, but lost track before the fear mounted that I would miss the call. I picked up the phone and placed it to my ear. A voice I felt I'd heard before, though one I couldn't quite identify spoke my name, flatly, no question mark.

"Speaking," I said. "Who is this?"

"Just your average sound effects guy," the man said, the last three words modulated in the manner of an anonymous documentary film subject, the pitch deepened dramatically and rendered mechanical.

"Donovan Foley," I said.

"At your service," he said.

"Just like that?"

"It's easy to reach out and touch someone, these days."

He asked if I knew how closely I was being watched.

"I've always assumed I was being watched. More with each passing year."

"But do you know the nature of the attention your searches have aroused?"

Foley proceeded to list the most sensitive terms from

my search history over the past few weeks. The most effective method to invite the scrutiny of various agencies was to search for ways to cover your tracks online, apparently.

"Who is watching?" I asked.

"Who isn't?" Foley said. "Vector, friends of Vector, computing enthusiasts, rogue elements within Vector, random hobbyists, an old friend, a stalker unrelated to your present predicament, gray hats, black hats, white hats, grey hats, Blanche, her assistant, elements in the underground film industry, members of the intelligence community."

"You said 'gray hats' twice."

"American and British," he said. "Keep in mind that in recent days alone you've been heavily researching serial murder, how repeat killers avoid detection, government surveillance, FBI protocol, and how to more effectively hide your IP, which you've done inconsistently, by the way. Not to mention your taste in pornography."

"None of that's illegal."

"It raises the eyebrow."

"Is that why you're calling?"

"I'm calling on behalf of an associate of mine. I'd go so far as to say on behalf of a friend."

I asked him to get to the point.

"The assertions concerning Bevacqua are…overblown. I'd like to set the record straight. In person."

I was made to understand (or led to believe) that our call was shielded from Vector's monitoring by someone "on the inside." Foley's instructions, if I agreed, were to head to the pallet in SANS's warehouse that awaited shredding, and to immediately start on this job as though the call had precipitated it. The pallet held 25 legal tote boxes with dimensions of 25" x 16" x 14," adding up to 1500 pounds in need of destruction.

"Why would I meet with a person who uses a public suicide to scare me off the trail?" I asked.

"The museum incident? Bevacqua had nothing to do with that."

"You're saying Fister was lying."

"Look at his name," Foley said. "Look at all the names. Vector Industries? Nothing to do with aircraft flight paths. What are they a vector of, do you think? Nothing good, I can assure you. They're a parasite that transmits other parasites, one that has been trying to groom you all along."

The phone nearly slipped out of my sweaty hand when I placed it in the base unit. I moved to the warehouse, stunned by recent developments. A new triangle had formed, or was forming, one defined in drastically different ways depending on who you asked. According to Vector, Foley was guilty—of what exactly? Fister insinuated Foley had stolen company property, and was implicated in something far worse for his association with Lucian Bevacqua. As far as the claims against Bevacqua— what proof had I seen? Disturbing films, certainly, but no evidence of his status as international snuff overlord. I had been in Foley's house, or a house used by Foley to lie low, and I'd seen no bodies, just a telescope and a bunch of jars. As for the jars themselves, what I had seen in them, briefly, was cast in doubt for various reasons. I agreed to meet Foley for the simple reason that I wanted to hear his story, his explanation, and to hear what he had to offer.

In the warehouse, my mind wandered while I drove a forklift to the next pallet in the shredding queue. I willfully ignored several safety tips for the operation of heavy machinery. Most forklifts are orange or yellow—I assume the warm colors are for visibility—Shred Authority Neighborhood Storage had a little green one. After inserting the twin forks under the pallet and engaging the lift cylinder, I: didn't check to see if the load was secure, accelerated blindly around corners, remained deliberately unaware of obstacles below and above, didn't perform any pre-op safety procedures, made extreme accelerations and decelerations, exceeded the speed of 6 m.p.h. (standard safe speed) and in fact floored the accelerator en route to one of SANS's truly massive Weima WL18 shredders, a dumpster-like affair next to a 9-step steel rolling ladder.

I turned on the Weima and, during warm-up, raced up the rolling ladder with tote box after tote box, throwing them in entire. Severely winded after about a dozen of the boxes, I paused to turn on the machine. As it kicked into action with a massive whir, I plodded up with the remainder of the boxes, tossing them into the rending maw. If not against procedure per se, this was inefficient and inappropriate use of company equipment. The cardboard tote boxes were ripped apart by the shredder's teeth, causing papers to fly into the air, some escaping the shredder itself and floating into other parts of the warehouse. Much of the paper was certainly pulled between the teeth and shredded by finer blades underneath, however. I picked up the pallet, considered de-nailing it, decided against, and tossed it into the

Weima's orifice. Wood cracked and shattered, sending fragments in all directions. I got the spins in a major way, and had to pause to catch my breath.

Returning to the forklift, I found a single piece of paper on the vinyl seat. It read, if one could say it was legible, if one could say it was *lisible*:

℺

Was this yet another variation on the little letter? According to an Internet search, the glyph was a "telephone recorder symbol," employed to signify the presence of telephone-related services or info in print, on billboards, and so on. Just as roadside signage alerted one to the presence of a rest area at a specific exit, the above symbol (in former times) signaled a public telephone. I was puzzled at the "recorder" phrasing, until I learned that one of Edison's innovations was to use the phonograph as a telephone recorder, using microscopic sound vibrations to record patterns in wax. By turning the paper 180 degrees, the meaning of the glyph changed (or did it?) to the astronomical symbol of conjunction, i.e. when two astronomical objects have the same ecliptic longitude or right ascension, whatever that meant. Two astronomical objects are in conjunction dependent on the observer's perspective, usually viewing from Earth. Just as the glyph's meaning appeared to change when I rotated the paper, the conjunction of astronomical bodies was similarly subjective at bottom. An additional meaning, though I despaired of ever discovering the intention behind any link in this chain of little letters, turned out to be what is known as a "rotated capital Q" a.k.a. a "signature mark" formerly used in bookbinding to differentiate new sections in a folio. A signature, like the trail left behind by a snail, or pieces of the body.

I looked at the symbol, watching it change, or perhaps willing it to do so.

The progression of the little letter from the moment I had first encountered it had, until now, been one of disintegration. The "ᗡ" or "circle joined with line" had become, separately, an "o" and "|", merging again into an "i" of sorts before morphing further. What was I to make of these symbols, divorced as they were from any meaningful context? I made my way to our NSA-approved, CSS-recommended, TAA compliant cross-cut shredder with Security Level P-7. A favorite of the military cryptologic community, this shredder was capable of turning a sheet of paper into 15,000 particles each measuring 1/32" x 3/16." A sheet turned into particles in this manner was technically unreconstructable. This shredder was special. I was unsure what I expected when inserting the found page in the cross-cut shredder's throat. The disturbed moan of an ancient deity? The terror-filled cries of millions of voices? Mournful ghost wails from an obscure corner of the nation? Tremors? The shrieks of desperate winged creatures homing in on my location with great speed?

The shredder took the page, transformed it into particles smaller than 1 millimeter by 5 millimeters, or 0.03125 inches by 0.1875 inches. This, in the jargon of the Secure Destruction Industry, is what is called "terminal destruction." Each particle is the size of a pencil mark; in fact, letters are reduced to mere mark. I considered the possibilities of the now-absent glyph. The symbol for astronomical conjunction, the rotated capital Q denoting a signature mark, and the telephone recorder glyph, drawn from the fields of astronomy (and astrology), bookbinding, and telephony, respectively. Clearly, each field was relevant to my search, but how?

Something appeared to rest on the intersection of bodies in space, the order of pages and sections in a text, and the movement of information through wires.

The call from Foley had rattled me, while also arriving accompanied by a sense of building pressure, a sense of inevitability. During the course of my research, I had discovered a town called Telephone, Texas. The town of Telephone, when considered in conjunction with Meridian, Texas and Waco, Texas, formed a loop of sorts, the center of which was a museum with the sinister vibe of science gone wrong in caliginous underground chambers. I thought about the children's game of Telephone, known as Chinese Whispers in the United Kingdom as far back as the 1960s and as Russian Scandal 100 years before that. Known by other names worldwide, the game would appear to illustrate the inherent slipperiness of language, the impossibility of "true" communication, the broken nature of discourse itself. Compare following phrases:

It's all Greek to me.

Es kommt mir Spanisch vor. (It's all Spanish to me.)

Czeski film—nikt nic nie wie. (A Czech film—nobody knows anything.)

I was the actor in a Czech film, or the unwilling subject of a documentary in another language.

By meeting Foley, was I coming closer to a tenuous grasp of anything? One of his utterances lingered in my mind: "Look at all the names." I thought about his name at length, attempted to keep it in my awareness against some form of resistance. Donovan Foley. The surname was apparently Irish, from incomprehensible earlier versions meaning "plunderer." I found a Foley, Alabama; a Foley, Florida; Foleys Minnesota and Missouri. "Folio" meant a sheet or leaf of paper, and later a volume thereof. Was I missing something? Reminders of the elusive and disputed psychological condition *folie à deux* occurred to me. Who were the likely candidates for a madness of two, a shared delusional disorder? And which pair could most effectively recruit another into a burgeoning *folie à trois*? Was it wise to enter an isolation chamber with Foley, thus giving him access to my mind, to my body? Or, having given Vector, via Blanche, unprecedented access, was I merely balancing the scales? Could a filmic or textual transmission create its own *folie à deux* in the mind of the viewer, in the mind of the reader? Of course—that would seem to be the goal of the whole enterprise. Was I missing something?

26

The building's facade was smooth concrete, giving it a bunker-like appearance, though oddly topped with an ornate cornice. Its function was announced in neon: "RUSSIAN, TURKISH, SAUNA, BANYA, TANNING, DAY SPA, MASSAGE." I entered the lobby via steps bordered by iron railings capped with tall spikes. An extended chime began as soon as the door closed behind me, gradually decreasing in volume until inaudible, giving the impression that the sound continued at a lower frequency. The man behind the front desk: portly, bearded, of indeterminately youngish age. I asked him the cost of admission.

"Forty dollars," he said.

I handed him my credit card. After glancing at the embossed letters of my name, he slid the card across the desk. He said my admission had been taken care of. He offered me vodka, which I accepted.

"This key," he said, holding one up to eye level, "This key is for your locker, which is through that door." He pointed to his left. "Inside is a towel, a robe, shorts, slippers, and flip flops."

I considered asking the man his name. He looked at me with the intense gaze of an untrained actor, or one who had undergone hypnosis. I moved toward the locker room, placing my hand on the door.

"One question," he said. "Do you have any medical issues."

"I don't think so," I said.

"High blood pressure or other cardiovascular conditions?"

"No."

The locker room was empty except for the kind of older gentlemen I'd expect to find in such a place. I took off my clothes and put on a bathing suit of thin black material with white netting inside. I considered the slippers and flip flops—the former were white and wrapped in plastic, while the latter were black and unwrapped. I rejected the slippers with some reluctance as likely to absorb moisture in the baths, debated what kind of cleaning regimen the flip flops were subjected to, and weighed the risks of wearing the flip flops versus going barefoot entirely. In the end I slipped them on, donned the robe, and opened another door, entering a corridor with tiled floor, wood-paneled ceiling featuring recessed lighting, and walls of wooden beams (likely cedar). Moments from film history occurred to me, specifically films containing steam rooms, of which there were many, including:

*S*H*E (1979)*
247°F (2011)
Steambath (1973)
T-Men (1947)
Eastern Promises (2007)
Spartacus (1960)
John Wick (2014)
Gorky Park (1983)
Goldeneye (1995)
House of Strangers (1949)
What Time Is It There? (2001)

One wonders about the frequency of sauna deaths in film, a phenomenon no doubt connected to vulnerability and the sound-dampening womb-like properties of the steam bath experience, as well as the obvious sexual pleasure linked to rising temperatures, relaxation, and the removal of clothing. I passed a series of beach chairs reclining in front of a row of television screens, one featuring a beweaponed soldier in a shaggy, red, faux-fur rocking chair, oscillating. No audio. A single man in a reclining chair watched the broadcast, a towel on his head. I found another door, entered it, and walked into a chamber of heat and lavender.

I sat down on one of the wooden benches lining the room and began sweating. My impression was one of repeatedly encountering different versions of the same man: graying hair, large gut, grizzled cheeks, taciturn. This latest one was differentiated by a dragon sleeve tattoo, the head and claw of which occupied his entire shoulder. In addition to the lavender, Eucalyptus and other aromatic shrubs played about my nostrils in a nearly visible fashion. This was the dry sauna, heated by radiators. Two women conversed on an upper row of benches; I tried to listen in on their conversation.

"...that's when she bumped into it," the first woman

said.

"A body?" the second woman asked.

"It just surfaced next to her."

"Doesn't look like it has hurt business much."

At this point, the women laughed uproariously and glanced in my direction. My heartbeat asserted itself at several points along my body. My lubricious coating became somehow cold, and I went from pleasantly lightheaded to, well, unpleasantly so. I exited the dry sauna, stepping into a wall of steam. This next room held a small crowd of men, women, and couples; sitting and prostrate, in various configurations. A few bath house attendants administered treatments to those stretched out on slabs. I took off my robe and focused on the effort required to take deep breaths of thick vapor. It was difficult to decide whether I felt the need to drink water or vodka—likely both. The people around me were conversing in a language or languages other than English or Russian. I could only compare it to someone with an American accent speaking Dutch, Danish, or some extinct Germanic variant at the edge of earshot—the intonations, rhythms, and gestures were familiar, yet everything save cognates was unintelligible. I located a bucket of water and ice which I emptied over my head.

A nearly endless succession of rooms followed. The robe had been left behind; my only possessions at this point were sandals, shorts, and the single locker key in their left front pocket. I doubted that my phone, secured in the locker, would have functioned at what felt like an extreme depth. Dizzy and weak, I lost track of how many rooms I had passed through: hot and dry, hot and steamy, warm and fragrant, hot and fragrant, warm and dry, hot and steamy yet again, shockingly cold. I dipped myself in frigid pools to the point of exquisite pain, relishing the brief clarity. Nevertheless, each seriate wave of dull heat encased my brain, slowed my plod. At length I found a sink in a hallway lit by blue light, filled a nearby pitcher, and drank from the brim. There was no need to urinate for the longest time—when I did, the fluid was dark, something between gold and Dijon.

I pictured spending sixty years exploring the baths, and still not exhausting the possibilities and interconnections therein. I struggled to think of a term other than labyrinthine. This was the Mammoth Cave of bathhouses: the longest bathhouse in the world, the one whose end no explorer could find. I lumbered along, seeking a bucket whenever I felt presyncope or whatever I was feeling. Temperatures ranged from maybe 35° in the cold pools to 200° or more in the banya. I became engrossed with patterns on mosaic tile floors. My mental record of turns taken was hopelessly jumbled. If forced to guess, I'd say I was being driven toward some central point, though this too could've been an illusion.

For a time, a repeated pattern of two right turns followed by a long straightaway were followed by two left turns and a straight stretch of similar length, suggesting the regular movement of a figure on a game board, e.g. an electronically manipulated snake image ingesting rows of eggs or other objects. Later, I became convinced that the frequency of left turns meant I should have already encountered my earlier path. Fleshy bathers passed me in the hallway on occasion, and I was tempted to shake one, to plead for directions to an exit. The crowds thinned, then disappeared. I lugged my body through room after room, beginning to wonder when I'd see daylight. I quit dallying in the hotter rooms, and didn't submerge myself except to dangle legs in cold pools and scoop water onto my head. In each room, I began to take note of a single individual. Not the same, yet similar. Each room featured a version, to my heat-befuddled brain, of the burly gentleman from before: paunchy, gray or graying, profoundly sad. I found that when I focused on this man, hurriedly giving him the eye in the sauna, a lingering glance in moments of cool respite, I became aware of another figure in the room, this one hovering on the edge of my vision. Whenever the periphery lost its peripheral status, all signs of the second figure disappeared.

It was only in what I later came to think of as the final room that the figure, in effect, materialized. How long had he been waiting here? Had his presence eluded me in earlier rooms? Upon entrance to this so-called final room, I walked into a wall of steam. Seating areas were cut into stone in a stairstep configuration, and covered with wooden slats, likely cedar; each of the levels was obscured by progressively more steam, and was therefore several degrees hotter. I considered what might happen to a person, sauna-trapped. If unhealthy enough, an infarction or appearance of a thrombus would be the likely and least unpleasant result. Failing such an event, dehydration could lead to renal failure. One way or another, following death, the body would proceed to fall apart.

I counted four levels of seating around the room's perimeter. Standing in the room's central point, I heard an odd sound, or rather a sound not odd in and of itself, but for its lack of connection to any apparent source. The sound I heard was that of a creaking door, specifically, what any viewer of television or film would recognize as a "creaking door sound effect," lasting at least five seconds and followed by the sound of a door closing. At the highest level of seating, in the room's corner, I discerned a pair of feet and legs, the latter covered by a white towel from the shins upward. Hands on knees, the outline of a torso—all other anatomical aspects were wreathed in steam. A mass of white mist billowed between me and the figure.

"I want to thank you for coming all the way down here," Donovan Foley said.

"If I'd known how far it was I might have reconsidered," I said.

"My thanks, nevertheless," he said.

"You said you wanted to correct the record." I said.

A sound resembling rotating helicopter blades filled the room. Or: the sound of large fans, turned on and off, recorded, distorted, and edited became incongruously audible in the underground space.

"You seem overeager," he said. "For us to proceed, there's something you have to do. You have to slow down. Doable?"

"Of course," I said.

[RESOUNDING CANNED LAUGHTER]

After an indeterminate amount of time had passed, during which I observed the silent room and its moving contents, Foley spoke again.

"Let's start with a question. Ask me anything, if you will."

"What do the little letters mean?" I asked.

"Well, I'd like to oblige this question, but a single question requiring multiple answers is hardly fair, is it?"

"What about the first one? The 'a,' or what looked like an 'a' on your lapel pin?"

"Bonus points for an excellent revision," he said.

Foley gave me two answers after all. The 'a,' or that which resembled an 'a' stood for *autre*, or "other" in another language. By the same token, the later 'o,' or that which et cetera, stood for "other," or *autre* in another language. Foley's lapel pin from the flight so long ago labeled him as other, among other things. At no point during our conversation was Foley's head and shoulder region unobscured by steam.

"Who are you?" I asked.

"Far too direct," he said. "I'm an editor, just like you."

"I'm not an editor," I said.

"On the contrary. Cutting and splicing celluloid is no different from shredding."

"I didn't think anyone used celluloid anymore."

"True. Though I've used it all," he said. "Now I work on nonlinear machines."

"Anyway, shredding isn't exactly editing. I'm just destroying the paper."

"Depends on your way of looking at things. Turning a piece of writing into particles or strips is merely inserting a great number of blank spaces into the text."

"I don't follow."

"Let's imagine we have a sheet of paper on which a single word has been typed."

[MEDIUM STUDIO AUDIENCE: EXTENDED CURIOUS "OOOH" SOUND]

A series of wavelike spasms took place in my lower alimentary canal.

"Let's say the word is 'mask.'"

[LARGE STUDIO AUDIENCE: WHISTLING AND CHEERING SOUNDS]

"OK," I said.

"Cutting the word in half, into 'ma' and 'sk,' is the insertion of one blank space. Cutting further, into four letters, results in three blank spaces. The letters themselves can be reduced to their constituent shapes, of course. And reduced even further, thereby generating exponential growth of blankness, like surface area."

"Odd you should use the word mask," I said.

"Is it?"

"What does Vector want?"

"They want—I should say—it wants to use you to destroy Bevacqua."

"What's your connection to Bevacqua?" I asked.

"Emissary. Collaborator. Friend."

"Friend?"

"A friend indeed. Bevacqua can be a friend to you. He can be your meal ticket, and much more besides."

"What would happen if I gave you the envelope Vector asked me to deliver?"

"Much suffering followed by certain death. Or uncertain death, whichever is worse," he said.

The word "ensorcelled" appeared to me, as if on a cue card, in blackletter typeface called Fraktur:

ensorcelled

A dizzy spell, if you will. A rerun of one of my episodes. (Pardon the puns.)

"Did you look at the names, as I suggested?" Foley asked.

"Yes. Which did you have in mind?"

"Fister, for example, wants to fuck you—not in the sense of brachioproctic insertion, but rather metaphorically."

"On behalf of Vector," I said.

[GONG EFFECT]

"Bingo."

"What about Blanche?"

"What about her?"

"Does she fall into Fister's camp?"

"Entertaining the idea provides you some enjoyment," Foley said. "Blanche is a true believer. What it is she actually believes is another question entirely."

[SOUND OF LARGE OBJECT FALLING INTO WATER]

I asked about Bevacqua's alleged production of snuff films, his involvement with the supply of these films to law enforcement agencies around the country.

[LAUGH TRACK OF CHILDREN GIGGLING]

"What's the scariest thing you can think of?" asked Foley. "Or, rather, what are the most reprehensible human actions outside of mass murder? You needn't answer, just hold it in your mind."

"OK."

"This is what Vector is insinuating. We've heard it all. One week it's this thing, another week it's the other. Fister isn't above smearing Bevacqua—a true artist, by the way—as an enigmatic figure with multiple aliases, a refugee of white Namibian extraction holding Swiss and South African passports last seen residing in Malaysia, a figure either formerly or currently involved in the international drug trade, gunrunning, and human trafficking, and now with numerous inscrutable links to various government agencies."

[SOUND OF AN OLD DOORBELL]

"And all of this is merely fantasy."

"Do you ever ask yourself why Vector approached you?" Foley asked.

I stood transfixed, no longer aware of my body, gazing up into the thick cloud from which the voice issued. Everything around us had fallen away, and I had the impression of being suspended over a massive vertical rock exposure. If I asked, would Foley show himself to me? If he were willing, I had an inkling who I would see gazing back.

27

Hours after the baths spit me out—dehydrated but with newfound knowledge—I returned to my apartment. I gorged myself on purified water, showered, heated leftovers. Having attended to physical needs, I entered my bedroom to find an unfamiliar manila folder on my desk. Inside the folder were several grainy color photographs with the look of surveillance footage stills:

Photo of a man behind the wheel of a car, reaching out the window toward the camera at an automated toll booth.

Photo of a woman and a man entering a truck stop, the former carrying a large, black bag.

Photo of the same man and woman in a hallway (hallway walls tiled in white, hallway floor tiled in brown).

Photo of the same man unclothed on the floor of a shower and surrounded by blood, his throat cut.

Photo of the man's upper torso, head, and throat, the latter slashed from ear to ear, rendering him nearly decapitated.

Photo of the same woman exiting the truck stop, still carrying the large, black bag.

Despite the quality of the photographs, I recognized the pair. Searching the internet for news of the slaying turned up the broad outlines. At some point during the last few days, they had arranged to meet at a rest area roughly 150 miles southwest of the city, a stop with separate parking lots for cars and big rigs. They had arrived in two cars, entered the convenience store portion of the rest stop, and headed toward the bathroom and shower area through a door in the back, a door through which only the woman had emerged some 30 minutes later. It was unclear how the woman—the suspect, *the likely assailant*—had absconded as both the car she parked at the scene (reported stolen from a nearby suburb three months prior) and the car belonging to the man—the victim, *the assailed*—were left behind. Information concerning the assailant's whereabouts was sought with great urgency; authorities assumed she had fled, had been helped to flee, either in a third car or in one of many semi-trailer trucks a.k.a. big rigs. The car formerly belonging to the assailed was registered to one Liam _______, a fact of no surprise. Blanche, of course, was the woman in question who had left Liam garroted to the point of near-decapitation on the shower floor.

As I read local news and police reports, my phone lit up and vibrated with a call from Blanche. I closed the browser and exited my apartment. It was time to enter a public space, a well-lit location surrounded by bystanders. It was time to reestablish contact with Foley.

28

A dream:

I found myself at an airport gate waiting to board. The seating area was nearly full—families abounded, and the young, the youthful, and the young at heart occupied space on the floor. A line of travelers across the room stood waiting for their boarding group to be called. I was content to sit and observe. One man performed a double take in my direction. He doubled the double gesture, resulting in two double takes or four ganders. He then feigned nonchalance by turning away, continuing, however, to glance with a slight turn of the head. The man appeared to grow agitated as the line inched forward. He stood close to a woman and child in front of him in line, seemingly willing to trample them to enter the plane. The mother only looked at me once, prompted by the frequent glances of the one behind her. He was familiar, to say the least. Familiar and exceedingly odd at the same time. His gaze had the look of someone judging a vast distance, or a vast depth. A ticket agent addressed me over this distance, asking if I was able to board. It would be a while before I adjusted to my situation. I picked up a fully lined matte ebony leather duffel bag ("An American Classic") with brass hardware, secret interior pocket, and single-letter embossed monogram, approached the ticket agent, handed over my boarding pass, and entered the jetway. One line became another and all I could think about was the word "eerie"—with its many vowels, and the letter "r" trapped inside.

29

My next destination was the city outskirts. "Outskirts," a pluralization of "outskirt," the singular term for an outer border we no longer use. Foley had made promises, claimed to disclose revelations, and while I didn't trust him completely, crime scene photos depicting a dead friend are just the thing to spur a leap of faith. According to Foley, Blanche was preparing to offer me a choice on Vector's behalf. I could don the blindfold and take Foley's place as the man of distorted visage, doing the bidding of Vector and Bevacqua, or I could take my chances and meet a fate similar to Liam's ugly end. Foley, however, suggested another path.

I considered taking the subway to the line's northwesternmost end before finding a taxi there because, in part, I thought underground transit might somehow thwart any attempt by Blanche or others to locate me via cell phone or public cameras. However, I couldn't shake the vision of Blanche journeying overland, following the path of the railway or heading it off on a lime green and ebony Kawasaki Ninja ZX-10, gunning for me. In a similar vein, I worried that any taxi I might select could be driven by a Vector plant. One after another, taxis sought me out: honking, waving, cutting off other drivers to scoop me up. I dodged traffic to cross the boulevard, catching sight of a parked cab with his light on. When I mentioned the name of the estate, he asked for an address or general directions rather than nodding ominously, an encouraging sign.

The driver was silent, his cab an official city cab barren

of ornament. I took a photo of his taxi license number and emailed it to myself with a certain sense of futility. If he were to deliver me to death, would this documentation yield results? Would strangers in masks torture me until I unlocked the phone, thereby allowing them to delete the email and attached photo? Is it protocol for police in this century to comb through the data generated during a victim's final days? Would the photo, if deleted, remain on servers in this country or another? Would Vector be able to gain access thereto via my mobile service provider? Should I then create a social media account, share the image in a publicly accessible manner, and change the password to something so lengthy it'd be nearly impossible to crack or remember? Would sending the image to a friend (did I have any left?), acquaintance, or relative bring scrutiny, suffering, or death upon them as well?

I glanced again at the driver's identifying information. Something about the shape of his name calmed me. We passed along bridges and under overpasses, passed trees, rivers, choked streams, bright and decaying shopping plazas. To keep the driver in view and lower my own visibility to those outside the vehicle I slumped in the back right seat to a degree I thought wouldn't cause alarm. After a time we left the freeway and trees cropped up in abundance. A two-lane highway with a number designation became a numberless two-lane, which in turn became a country road. When we came upon a small bridge with a traffic light above it, wide enough for traffic to cross in one direction at a time, leading to a so-called F.M. (Farm to Market) road, a dirt road with a gravel dusting, the driver balked until I offered an extra twenty in cash for the inconvenience.

A wrought-iron gate at least eight feet high became visible off the shoulder as we arrived at a lavish entrance. It belonged to what one might call the neo-Gothic style, with leaves, scrolls, flowers, disturbingly rictal faces. The gate rested on two embellished hexagonal bases, and rose in six-lobed pillars linked by an intricate arch topped by sharp finials. I noticed cameras at intervals along the gate, sun-shielded lenses peaking out of orbs designed to match the scrollwork. Also apparent were a series of so-called "voided lozenges," a lozenge being essentially a heraldric diamond shape, the voided aspect meaning a hole existed in the center of the shape. I heard tinkling of piano notes—Brahms, of course. I paid the driver and was alone at the gate.

As I considered whether to try numbers on a keypad near the entrance, or to press one of the buttons marked "HELP" or "CALL," the gate buzzed and swung slowly open. I paused, looked at the nearest watchful orb, vainly trying to read its surface, then slipped through as the gate began to close behind me. It closed with the usual metallic sound. With no discernible means of exiting the grounds, my first thoughts involved the subjective experience of being ripped apart by trained dogs. Shredded. Perhaps I should have armed myself. But against what, exactly?

The forested estate was immaculate, oddly dotted with statues and fluted plinths. The cost of upkeep must've been enormous; the staff required would amount to a small army. Nevertheless, I saw no one at first, and the only sounds were songbirds and the wind. The first sculpture I came across resembled a fragment: a damaged marble head of enormous size on a pedestal. Missing was a single ear and much of the head above the Roman hairline. I say the piece resembled a fragment because I was unsure of its status as replica or original. If a replica, surely the head was a "complete" replica of the original fragment. If an original, could it not be a finished fragment, and therefore completely incomplete? The breaks were too clean to be simply a damaged whole. In any case, a number of so-called fragments have been deliberately fashioned in several genres. A fragment isn't merely something that appears unfinished. The very idea presumes the existence of some sort of whole. Choosing to stop therefore meant a work had arrived at completion.

The next piece I encountered was a marble hand on a pedestal the scale of which suggested association with the enormous head. All fingers of the hand were folded down save the index, which pointed skyward at a slight angle. It was also white marble or a material intended to imitate the appearance thereof.

The path bifurcated, and I took the curve, not prepared to arrive at the mansion's front door. I attempted to picture Bevacqua. Might he sport an eyepatch, a moustache, a feeding tube? What would be his means of conveyance? According to Foley, Bevacqua aimed to offer me a deal. If Vector desired my servitude in their employ, in place of Foley, what did Bevacqua desire? I imagined a scenario in which I was offered the technology not only to obscure my face, but to assume any face I desired, a technology that delivered a pleasure so great as to be habit-forming. Pleasures—monetary, prurient, and otherwise—occurred to me in great number: entering your neighbor's home wearing the face of your neighbor's spouse, entering a jewelry store projecting the face of the proprietor, entering a crowded nightclub with the face of a celebrity, entering the John F. Kennedy Conference Room a.k.a. the White House Situation Room having assumed the face of the Assistant to the President and Chief Digital Officer. Perhaps Foley wanted out, wanted to step down to retain his humanity. Perhaps he wanted to remember what it felt like to walk the earth with a single face. Perhaps we'd establish a rotating stewardship of the device, if it were simply a device, or the role would be passed on. I considered what my answer would be to an offer conveying power of this magnitude, even for, say, a 27-month stint in the vein of the Peace Corps. If the position were a permanent one, would I turn it down?

The well-manicured path traced a subtle arc. In the distance, I heard the revving of a motorcycle engine and thought of Blanche. I began jogging. I passed: three agonal marble figures attempting to defend themselves from an attack by marble snakes, passed reclining nudes in bronze, terracotta elephants, limestone statuettes, apparent replicas of Greek funerary monuments, colossi, emperors, stone and glass mosaics, quotidian objects of cement, of fiberglass, of painted stainless steel, statuary covered with algae as though recently retrieved from the depths, polished granite furniture, polychrome aluminum figures that appeared to move. Coming to another fork, my choice was to continue the gentle curve that seemed to ring the estate or to make a hard left toward what I assumed would be the mythopoeic filmmaker's mansion. I chose the latter, and due to a mixture of curiosity and fatigue, slowed down to observe the sculptures that flanked the path in a staggered pattern: a patinated bronze gallows, marble fragments either armless, legless, or headless, idealized nude torsos, five-legged lamasus, a clockwork bull with innards revealed, a writhing pile of larvae, a black cube, a torqued ellipse, and other assorted and hybrid terrors. I heard the clang of the entrance gate in the distance and began to run.

The mansion, creaky from age and neglect, became visible ahead. I could make out a fountain, wall-climbing ivy, a slate roof, a weathervane-topped cupola featuring a bird of prey, and a façade that appeared symmetrical at first, until small details tugged at the attention—a window, a shutter, a door—hinting at a form slightly askew. Turning slowly toward the mansion, I observed a helicopter in the distance cut through a meaningless cloud, its spinning blades turning cumulus to shreds.

Bevacqua, I now knew, wanted to make me a star. As I continued to move toward the structure ahead, the shape of the grounds—a circular path bisected by a straight one—occupied my thoughts. I paused to take in the path behind me. No sign of human presence, and no sound. I realized what had been troubling me: the shape formed by the path and the series of objects along it, if seen from above, betokened what you might call a bar sinister, a universal no, a sign of prohibition, a no sign, an interdictory circle, a no symbol. If seen from above, the shape of the path pointed toward a vast negation.

30

The massive front door to the mansion was unlocked. I entered without hesitation, afraid that Blanche could be close behind. I heard no further engine sounds, and assumed she had walked the motorcycle onto estate grounds and proceeded on foot. Or perhaps the sounds of revving and the clanging gate were related to some third party?

Inside was the powerful, comforting smell that old houses have: a mixture of dust, sweetness, a ghost of smoke from hundreds of hearth fires, odorous molecules from meals gone by, something once trapped in the ductwork. Closing the front door behind me encapsulated everything. The hardwood flooring somehow absorbed my every step. I wondered what kind of mysteries had been spilled onto the floor over the years: cold frothy milk, wine, vomit, pet urine, hot blood?

Don't think the place wasn't elegant—it was. Its age, however, increased the likelihood that someone had died there. The foyer was dominated by a chandelier that cast low light in all directions. A staircase extended into darkness above—I couldn't see the other end. Open hallways to what looked like a sitting room and a library were visible to my left and right. Straight back was a passage that eventually broke in two directions, a long, narrow table covered with decorative objects visible in the distance. Despite the lit chandelier, I wondered if anyone was home, since the place was filled with a silence that didn't seem temporary. I entered the library, or what could generously be called such—more so a reading room—and flipped a light switch.

The room was designed to pull at one, its couches, chairs, and ottomans exuding comfort. A long window overlooking the grounds lined one wall, under which a narrow recessed day bed recalled something you'd see on a ship. A white flag bleached from years in the sun was in a frame—it was recognizable as American, barely, though with only 48 stars. An aged globe in a curved three-legged floor stand was in the corner. I approached and gave it a spin. It moved silently, and I plopped a finger down, the globe coming to rest on a country in Africa I had never heard of, Bechuanaland. It was bordered by South Africa, which I had heard of, South-West Africa, and Rhodesia—Northern and Southern Rhodesias, no less. I realized I was looking at a fairly old globe. A handful of recognizable shapes and names were present, but many were prefixed: French this, Belgian that, Anglo-Egyptian Sudan. Italian Somaliland and Spanish Sahara. Certain names tickled the ear in a way that suggested they had only subtly changed. Tanganyika?

I moved to a wall of books, remembering that Bevacqua was rumored to have been born in Namibia, likely of Dutch or British abstraction. Foley had told me this. I returned to the globe, but there was no Namibia there.

One bookcase was packed so tightly as to form a faded multicolor wall of leather. Another wall was paperbacks, mysteries, black with garish lettering in orange or red, trench coats, femmes fatales, smoking strangers with hidden faces, a revolver on a table, a martini, a pair of handcuffs, a blindfold. I began to flip through the mysteries, sure that I'd find a significant photograph or note stuck between pages, or even a book that had been hollowed out to conceal something of worth. I heard a creaking sound from the direction of the foyer, and returned the book I was holding to the shelf. It was titled *The Circular Staircase*, which I wondered whether the mansion contained.

The foyer was unchanged, no one in sight, and the top of the stairs remained invisible from my vantage point. Something about stairs is inherently frightening, whether going up or coming down. Going down, there's always the moment after you've taken the first step or two, when you aren't out of range of a pusher and can feel a tingling, a tightness in the shoulders and lower back. Climbing stairs generates a similar issue: you're vulnerable from behind, and there is the potential that someone could launch themselves at you from above, or toss something heavy down. The point being, you can't look in two directions at once.

I passed the stairway to enter the dining room, circled a long table of dark wood that would seat at least fifteen, noticed a fireplace that, though clean, had been recently used, and entered the kitchen. The refrigerator is what stopped me—it was mint green, looked like it weighed 300 pounds, had one of those metal latching handles, smooth surfaces, rounded edges, and said "Philco" in large silver lettering with liberal spacing:

P H I L C O

Before I could consider opening it, I heard a telephone ringing somewhere close. If you haven't experienced it, the sound of an old telephone ringing in an empty or nearly empty house—and "ringing" literally, as in the mechanism of a hammer striking a bell inside the thing—can be terrifying. After remaining immobile for a number of rings, I left by the kitchen's second door, which connected to the hallway at the other end of the foyer. The sound was coming from down the hall, but I couldn't bring myself to seek the source. Was the ringing echoed by another telephone somewhere in the structure? If so, was the timing of the sound just imperceptibly off?

The ringing stopped, and I found my gaze drawn down the hallway. An odd portrait of a woman adorned the wall, her smeared gray and white form emerging out of a black background. The ethereal torso was largely transparent, topped by a head and coiffure that were an undifferentiated mass; the woman's outline was that of half a bowling pin, or a white chess pawn. Her nose and mouth did not align, contributing to the disjointed appearance. Two dark eyes looked out of the thick impasto of the face. Tiny white writing in the frame's lower left identified the subject as "Mlle Suzy Solidor," who I seemed to recall as harboring the ambition to become the most painted woman in the world, in her time at least.

The phone began to ring again, and I moved toward the sound if only to end its horrible reverberation. The phone was clunky and black, with a large base, rotary dial, and holstered receiver. It sat on an end table next to a plush, mustard-colored cocktail chair in a dark room whose other features included a lamp, sewing machine, and another painting that had escaped my notice upon entry. The cliché is that the ringing of a telephone can be insistent. On the contrary, the sound was just a response to stimulus, an automatic process, a repetition like breathing or beating of the heart. I picked up the receiver, careful to keep the mouthpiece away from my face.

"Hello," I said.

"Stop skulking about and come upstairs," a man said on the other end of the line. His voice had an edge to it that stopped just short of gravelly.

"Who is this?"

"The Caesarion of Snuff."

"The who?"

"The most acclaimed film director you've never heard of. Get the fuck upstairs."

I considered my options. I could exit the mansion, attempt to flee, and risk evisceration or worse by Blanche, I could keep poking around and risk the ire of the man upstairs, or I could follow his instructions. Why had I come to Bevacqua's mansion in the first place? To save myself, out of desperation, as a means of satisfying my own curiosity. Turning back would be impossible, akin to driving to Niagara Falls, parking, using the restroom, purchasing a souvenir toothpick holder, and leaving without witnessing the flow of up to 225,000 cubic feet per second.

I was able to locate Bevacqua's sitting room on the third floor because it was the only illuminated room on that level. The first thing the director said when I entered was, "I'm stronger than I look."

He didn't look very strong, it's true. You'd be forgiven for assuming he might resemble a cartoon villain, open cape of flowing red and black, demonic, leaking venom, but he looked like the old man I supposed he was. The question, then, if Bevacqua was stronger than he looked, was whether he was only a bit stronger than he appeared or inordinately so. He looked about seventy, though whether this was accurate or the result of hard living I couldn't tell. He had been a dapper fellow at one point, and perhaps still was. His deep-set eyes, thick, swept-back hair, angular features, oversized glasses, and tailored suit created a resemblance to a certain weather-beaten character actor with a cult following. A slender tube ran from his right nostril, disappearing under his collar. I was in awe.

"Make yourself at home," Bevacqua said, pointing to a sofa opposite his chair.

Again I did what I was told, this time with the strange feeling that I could stretch out on the sofa, stare at the ceiling or close my eyes, reveal secrets untold even to myself.

"You move like an actor," Bevacqua said.

"Thanks, I guess."

The atmosphere shifted from easy confidentiality to one of slight menace.

"You've been auditioning since you walked on my property. Technically since much earlier."

"Since when?" I asked.

"Then again, everyone is auditioning at all times."

"Auditioning for?"

"It's not what they're auditioning for," Bevacqua said. "It's that everyone is *being auditioned*, in the present moment at least."

"In the present moment?"

"Nowadays. In cities, your movement, your image is captured from nearly every angle by public, private, and commercial surveillance. Even in rural areas, people without a cell phone, laptop, or flatscreen connected to the Internet are few and far between. Last I heard, over 91% of Americans owned a cell phone."

"And you listen to them, watch them?" I asked.

"I have a staff that watches for me, edits, collates, curates. I give them direction, and they provide me with a menu of options."

"How would you describe your tastes?" I asked.

"You've seen my films. The word 'dark' is overused, in my view. When I get my staff to cull through years of raw footage, I instruct them to find something I can use. I want them to bring me something filmic."

I asked Bevacqua about his staff, and how Foley fit into the structure. He described Foley as one of the most exceptional foragers of video footage he had ever known, and an adept performer.

"But what he does isn't acting, exactly," he said. "Foley can walk into a room, and just stand motionless—it's impossible to look away. He knows that when you don't know what to do, it's best to do nothing. It's a gift."

"And he's your right-hand man?" I asked.

"No one is indispensable."

When I asked him about the old objects throughout his home, Bevacqua said he had bought the mansion from an even older man opposed to the passage of time. The seller had lived there since the 1950s, and preserved every possible element from that era.

"Including the globe?" I asked.

"Actually, that one in particular was a childhood toy

of mine," he said.

"Where was your childhood?"

"All over, and in Namibia."

A long silence fell—the lights seemed to dim, as though a sun separated from us by an unnoticed window had gone behind a cloud.

"The wiring in this place," Bevacqua said. "It's dreadful."

He asked me if I'd like to see some paintings he'd acquired. He led me to a curtained wall and pulled a golden cord. The three paintings behind the curtain, he said, belonged to the era preserved by the house and were of a piece with the depiction of Suzy Solidor that had entranced me so.

"This one is called *Head of Woman*," he said, pointing to a severely distorted head and upper torso smeared as though a thumb or other object had been dragged across the cheek and mouth. The woman's nose occupied roughly a third of her face. A faint aura that could have been her hair surrounded the head.

"This one is called *Lying Figure*," he said, gesturing toward a prone man on either the outline of a bed or simply a frame, his smudged face buried in a pillow or a book. A kind of chassis surrounded the bed, isolating it in space.

"And you might know what this one is called," he said, pointing to a painting of Donovan Foley sitting on a throne. Suit and tie, white frame, black background, face gone.

"By the way," Bevacqua said, "the word 'audition' didn't always mean what we take it to mean, but merely referred to the power of hearing, the auditory. The way 'cognition' refers to thinking."

He had the habit of pressing his fingertips together for emphasis, and did this repeatedly as he spoke. He paced in an animated fashion, almost as if he might begin dancing at any moment. I asked Bevacqua if he knew whether Blanche was on her way to murder me.

"Have you ever been in therapy?" Bevacqua asked.

"Briefly, but I quit when my life improved," I said.

"I can tell you what my two psychiatrists told me. You're remarkably well adjusted, considering. Your fears aren't rational, but are likely stress related. You aren't suffering, in the clinical sense, from a delusion of persecution. You don't, as far as I can tell, attribute grandiose meaning to insignificant objects, remarks, events, or symbols."

"What does this have to do with my question?" I asked.

"Blanche wants the best for you, in her own way. If I'm wrong, she'll gut you and bury your body in the desert where Idaho, Nevada, and Oregon meet," he said.

"Why would you be wrong?"

Bevacqua instructed me to follow him down a softly lit hallway, and opened the door to a red room: a sumptuous home theater with red and gold walls, lights along the floor, several rows of red theater seats. Off to the side was a lectern housing a computer and controls, presumably for the digital projector overhead that pointed toward a massive screen.

I considered Bevacqua's remark about having two psychiatrists, which brought to mind a television show on the model of the 1960s sitcom *My Three Sons* or even the one from the late 1980s called *My Two Dads*. Something in the vein of *My Two Shrinks*, in which two colleagues in the field of psychiatry learn that they've been treating the same patient. After the patient's death, the two doctors bond over shared experiences and gradually abandon the principle of patient-doctor confidentiality when they discover a shocking secret.

"Front and center," Bevacqua said, gesturing toward the first row of seats, consisting of five red armchairs. He approached the lectern and began typing. As soon as I sank into the middle chair, the lights dimmed and the projector kicked on.

It became clear that the screen in front of me displayed the content of Bevacqua's screen at the lectern, currently a command line of white text on a black background. He typed a series of instructions, including "location," which launched a map program.

He typed "Kuala Lumpur," which brought a map of the highway-ringed Malaysian city and its outskirts into view. "Kuala Lumpur International Airport" shifted the view south, revealing several terminals, including one shaped like an X. Terminal 2 hove into view, swarming with red icons, many of them moving.

"This is the airport in real time," Bevacqua said. "The red dots are visual sources, mostly mobile phones." I asked myself if this could be real.

"The computing power necessary to display this is immense. Right now I'm logged into a virtual machine in a Utah data center. *The* data center—the one storing quintillions of bytes."

Further typing generated an input field with hours and minutes, which Bevacqua adjusted backward.

"What you're about to see hasn't hit the news yet," he

said.

Footage from a crowded boarding area filled the screen. I watched as a stout man wearing a baseball cap, sunglasses, and leather jacket separated from the mass. A backpack hung by one shoulder strap. In a motion nearly too quick to notice, a briskly moving woman approached the man, grabbed him from behind, and held a cloth over his face for a few seconds. She released him and hurried away at the same pace. I could hear Bevacqua typing behind me.

Cut to the clearly disoriented man stumbling toward a ticket agent. Cut to the interior of an ambulance, the man's pained, upturned face filling the screen. Cut to footage of a post-mortem examination in progress.

"Who is that?" I asked.

"That was the half-brother of a well-known despot in the region," he said.

"Which one?"

"You'll find out if you pass a television or read the news any time soon."

A grainy still image filled the screen: a young woman, dark hair cut in a fringe, with dark, almost black lipstick and a long-sleeved white shirt printed with the letters "LOL." An icon for the twenty-first century.

Bevacqua explained that she was the killer, or one of them, and that the prevailing theory was that she was an operative sent by the dictator to off his estranged half-brother. He also told me what the news would later reveal: she and one other woman were unwitting killers, having been convinced to take part in what they were told was a game show centered around pranks. Their first two "targets" were actually operatives pretending to be airport travelers—the camera crew was also in on the plot. The women had been "dared" to squirt water into the faces of the first two travelers, before being presented with the third, actual victim. At some point Bevacqua interrupted himself, as though remembering a forgotten detail.

"Now for something equally beautiful," he said.

Further hospital room footage filled the screen, this time of a pregnant woman, legs splayed, face strained, surrounded by medical staff in scrubs, hair nets, and face masks, exhorting her to push as hard as she could when she felt a contraction, harder, harder, come on, inhale, long and hard, don't exhale, as hard as you can, and so on. From his commentary, I gathered that the father was filming.

A head emerged, a corded neck, an entire baby, purple and gray, which was briefly placed on the mother's stomach to much relief and merriment, then taken away for cleaning.

"She was born this century," Bevacqua said. "Which is why her footage is decent, digital, and more comprehensive." Cut to girl in a high chair, single candle in a cupcake. Cut to a later birthday, slightly larger cake surrounded by toddlers. Cut to footage of child undergoing tonsillectomy. Cut to footage of a soccer match. Cut to footage of teenager completing equation at chalkboard, bloodstain spreading on white pants before her panicked exit to general laughter. Cut to the interior of a Mexican restaurant, singing waitstaff encircling the table as one singer smeared whipped cream on the young woman's nose. Cut to footage of a cyclist on a sunny, forested trail—she looks toward the voice of the one filming her, looks at the camera and smiles.

"What happened to her?" I asked.

"Nothing yet. She's currently pre-med, though college students tend to change their majors at least three times over the course of their career, on average."

"And this is a real person's life, slices of it, all genuine?"

"I wanted to show you a happy ending," Bevacqua said.

"A happy ending through violation."

"Perhaps. But I'm a minor violator. My violations are minor, I mean, of course. I merely sift through what has been collected and preserved for years."

Bevacqua argued that since he produced art out of the personal data, rather than used it to find and imprison potential transgressors, that his motives were pure. I saw his point, in a way.

There are two main types of the nerve agent VX, American and Russian, and quantities of less than a drop, 0.050 ml, are deadly in under fifteen minutes. It is tasteless and without odor. Bevacqua said he preferred non-actors to actors, and even better than the performances of non-actors were the performances of those who didn't know they were being recorded.

"Compare the record of this woman's life with that of someone born today," he said. "A digital record much fuller and more realized, approaching complete."

"Approaching complete," I said.

"Nearly 99 percent complete, where audio is concerned. Excellent video coverage in urban areas, in front of laptops, and on the couch in front of smart TVs. Video is limited by the need for some upright camera apparatus—these gaps will be addressed by current and future product lines, no doubt."

"What else?"

"They—yes, 'They' with a capital 'T'—collect all the digital detritus, the so-called digital pocket litter which constitutes a life. Internet searches, travel plans, purchases, conversations, text messages, emails. All movement in space, all language produced—it's in storage. Searchable, but not to worry—no one is actively looking."

"I'd think searching audio would be time-consuming," I said.

"You'd be right, but machine transcription of audio is becoming more sophisticated all the time. The data center, and others we don't know about, is building a single massive text, one that will increase by orders of magnitude with each passing year."

Bevacqua's words produced the effect of a puzzle piece fitting into place. Not the final piece, not the penultimate, not even close, but the puzzle piece whose arrival suggested what part of the final image might look like. A single vast, expanding text, consisting of all the language produced in America—this text, in a sense, was America itself. America, its history, its language would be unreadable, at least to an individual.

I asked again how Blanche fit in, asked how much I had to fear.

"You ask her," Foley said, and exited the theater.

31

The lights came on, and I turned in my plush chair to watch Bevacqua leave. I saw no sign of him, but there in the back row was a familiar face.

"Don't get up," Blanche said, making her way down the red velvet steps. She was wearing a distressed black Moto jacket from Saint Laurent. I asked her if I should be worried.

"Of course not," she said. "You're referring to Liam, I assume."

I nodded. She wasn't carrying a weapon that I could see, unless it was a knife in a shoulder holster. I remained seated as she approached my armchair, mulling over what I'd be willing to do to her if she moved to disembowel me, how I would do it.

"I know you and Liam weren't really friends," she said.

"That's not exactly—"

"I know you don't have any friends to speak of. I know your whole history. Well, most of it."

I noticed a book sticking out of the pocket of her Moto jacket, title facing her body.

"What's that?" I asked. She handed over the heavy volume:

Bloodstain Pattern Analysis with an Introduction to Crime Scene Reconstruction

The authors of this textbook were named Gardner and Bevel, two utilitarian names that called implements to mind and sounded somehow unreal.

"Pretty bold to be carrying that around," I said.

"Should *I* be worried?"

"I wouldn't know."

Blanche surprised me by saying she wanted to apologize. Not for killing an acquaintance of mine, someone she claimed deserved it on many levels, but for following me for so long. She admitted that Vector ordered her to observe me for months before approaching me at the screening of *Pupfish*. She wasn't surprised when I said I already knew. She also apologized for staging her apartment, filling it with serial killer literature.

"They never interested you?" I asked.

"They did, though perhaps not to such a degree. Their golden age is over."

When I asked what she meant, Blanche responded that serial killings had been in major decline since the 80s or 90s. There were fewer serial killers, and the public was less excited by them. Advances in law enforcement methods, collaboration across state lines, and new technologies, above all, had contributed as well.

"Why pretend to have such an odd obsession?" I asked.

"Your profile suggested it would pique your interest," she said.

Blanche placed her motorcycle boot on the chair cushion between my legs. On some other day and under other circumstances I would have perhaps been intensely aroused, but I couldn't shake intrusive thoughts as to where she may have stepped.

"You did kill him."

"Like I said, he was asking for it," she said. Her boot inched forward, putting pressure on my genitals. "It's tough playing both sides."

"Or more than two," I said. "What did he do?"

"He was on Vector's payroll because of information he had. He asked for too much from someone very high up."

"Fister?"

"Higher still. Fister is just the CEO. He answers to the board of directors."

"Assuming I believe you, why are you here?" I asked.

"To apologize, truly. And to make sure you don't get spooked and do something rash."

"So, Vector wanted to use me to get to Liam, or to Foley?"

"Both, ideally," she said. "Since Foley has now completely disappeared."

I asked what the real relationship between Vector and Bevacqua was.

"Mutual wariness. Collaboration when their goals coincide. Bevacqua is an artist of great eminence. You should be flattered he has taken an interest in you."

She said that Bevacqua had created films on commission for prime ministers, presidents, queens, former presidents, dictators, supreme leaders, CEOs, empresses, philanthropists, grand dukes, magnates, tycoons, political donors, princesses regent, chief technology officers, investors, heiresses, socialites, sultans, emperors, *o le ao o le malos*, governors-general, chairmen, princes regent, kings, heirs, chieftains, entrepreneurs, emirs, co-princes, sovereigns, and managing directors of the IMF. Short films, mostly, as his time was not without limit. She said that for all his resources, he was only one man, and that Vector was prepared to offer me substantial rewards for my continued service.

Blanche asked if she could provide me with a ride. I watched her expression oscillate between menace and charm. She brought her face close to mine, and though her breath smelled of mint and lavender, as she exhaled I could only think of contagion. Simply breathing releases tiny droplets with more flu viruses than a human sneeze. Human speech, too, is a reliable producer of virus-filled aerosol particles.

My eyes fell to the t-shirt under her Moto jacket, and the text printed on it. It read "Three Dots and a Dash," which I happened to know was Morse code for the letter "V." The layers were making my head spin. You had words (spelled out) which referred to coded symbols, which stood in for a single letter. When I told Blanche I'd like to stay put for a while, she leaned over and kissed me forcefully on the mouth. V for victory.

32

The room, incidentally, was a duplicate in nearly every respect of the home theater inside the White House, site of screenings of such classic fare as *The Collector* (1965), *Twisted Nerve* (1968), *Enemy of the State* (1998), *What the Peeper Saw* (1972), *The Night Visitor* (1972), *Groundhog Day* (1993), *The Man Without a Face* (1993), *A Man of No Importance* (1995), *Fallen* (1998), *8MM* (1999), *The Thirteenth Floor* (1999), *Network* (1976), *The Shootist* (1976), *Silent Movie* (1976), *The Deep* (1977), *Orca* (1977), *United 93* (2006), *The Lincoln Conspiracy* (1977), *Murder by Death* (1976), *Black and White in Color* (1976), *Nuclear Tipping Point* (2010), *Boys from Brazil* (1978), *Phantom of the Opera* (1943), *Phantom of the Opera* (1925), *Phantom of the Opera* (1962), *Dracula* (1979), *The Picture Show Man* (1977), *The Marriage of Maria Braun* (1979), *Night of the Iguana* (1964), *When Time Ran Out* (1980), *Strangers on a Train* (1951), *Throw Momma from the Train* (1987), *The Flim Flam Man* (1967), *Airplane!* (1980), *The Mirror Crack'd* (1980), *The Mirror Crack'd* (1980), *Deathtrap* (1982), *Evil Under the Sun* (1982), *I Ought to Be in Pictures* (1982), *The Sound of Music* (1965), *Author! Author!* (1982), *From Russia with Love* (1963), *Salò, or the 120 Days of Sodom* (1975), *It's a Wonderful Life* (1946), *Cannibal Holocaust* (1980), *Trading Places* (1983), *Gorky Park* (1983), *Iceman* (1984), *Funny Face* (1957), *Broadcast News* (1987), *The Dead* (1987), *That's Entertainment, Part II* (1976), and of course, the first film screened, *The Birth of a Nation* (1915).

Though frequently reported, Woodrow Wilson probably didn't say of the film that it was like "writing history with lightning." Wilson never said this, and he likely didn't approve of the film, either. If history were ever to be written with lightning, however, which is to say electronically, America would have to wait nearly a century from Wilson's presidency before this could take place. If history were written with lightning, it was being written in Utah, in the so-called Intelligence Community Comprehensive National Cybersecurity Initiative Data Center.

I approached the lectern-housed computer, slid out the keyboard tray, and moved the mouse until the screen awoke. The desktop was clean except for a single text file and a browser icon in the shape of a globe, the continents delineated in a lime-like monochrome I thought of as "computer green." I opened the browser.

Loading relay information.

Testing network settings.

Circuit for this site: This browser -> France (57.275.43.247) -> Latvia (39.192.238.264) -> Netherlands (53.35.61.227 -> The Internet

You are now free to browse the Internet anonymously.

I maximized the browser window, which was relatively small, and was greeted with the following message: "Maximizing your browser can allow websites to determine your monitor size, which can be used to track you. We recommend that you leave browser windows in their original default size."

The text file was a manual of sorts, containing a series of instructions, keywords, shortcuts. It held a website address that was mostly numbers, which I entered into the browser. This was the search page for the massive Utah server. Search fields included:

NAME
DATE OF BIRTH
PLACE OF BIRTH
MAILING ADDRESS
PHONE
EMAIL ADDRESS
LOCATION
SOCIAL SECURITY NUMBER
DRIVER'S LICENSE NUMBER
PASSPORT NUMBER
KNOWN ASSOCIATES

Searching by any of these criteria gave one access to all the rest, as well as a splash page with archival and current footage of the subject, if any. The most striking aspect of the information at my fingertips was its nearly complete banality. Within minutes, I could tell you Ben Affleck's current location (Pacific Palisades, California) and his latest purchases at Gelson's Supermarket (kale, protein powder, and a 3-pack of vanilla Kaopectate). I was granted an exclusive live view of Miley Cyrus's inscrutable face, alone in the back of a limousine, to a soundtrack of Debussy. It took me a while to even find a "nude celeb," the viewing of which felt exceedingly banal. I searched for old friends, the ex I hadn't seen in years, my high-school sweetheart—it turned out that everyone had grown older.

I typed the president's name, attempted to retrieve

footage from inside the White House, to no avail. Recalling that Michael Bloomberg's social security number had once been leaked online, I found and entered the digits, bringing up a menu of the former mayor's homes in Colorado, Bermuda, The Hamptons, London, and so on. Footage from inside his limestone mansion on the Upper East Side yielded overhead camera views from a number of mostly empty rooms, footage of a housekeeper on a smoke break, a head-on shot of an immense Sunpan Modern Bugatti Grain Leather Sofa in white, the vantage point suggesting a nearby smart TV as the source of the footage, camera view from inside a private elevator, camera views from five flights of stairs the mayor claimed to use in lieu of the elevator, close-up footage of the man himself, head framed by white tile, a small soft blue painting glass-protected against moisture over his shoulder, his face contorted in some act of physical exertion.

I typed in "Donovan Foley" and received a handful of exact matches: a Donovan Foley in Heidelberg, South Africa, in Madera, California, in Peabody, Massachusetts, in Saint Paul, Minnesota, in Minneapolis, Minnesota, in Redford, Michigan. The middle names, when present, varied. I checked them all, only to find a farmer, mechanic, accountant, a pilot, the self-employed, the unemployed, or the indeterminate. Image and video confirmed their relative normalcy. Expanding parameters to include occurrences of the sequence "Donovan Foley" within longer names yielded a Denise Donovan Foley, a Sharon Donovan Foley, a Charles Donovan Foley, a Meghan Donovan Foley, none of which intrigued. I noticed, however, a Jack Donovan Foley whose splash page featured an old-timey sepia photo and no video footage, which made sense when I noticed he had died in 1967 in Lebanon, Kansas.

Reginald Fister had claimed Foley was born in Kansas, near Lebanon, at the site of the geographic center of the contiguous United States. It seemed odd that another Foley would have died the same year, though not impossible. His age (born in 1891) suggested this might be Foley Senior. Under "known associates" was a John Donovan Foley, born in 1967. His splash page revealed exactly nil; each field was followed by a blank. Where an identifying photo should be was a gray square.

Returning to Foley Senior only complicated things further: also under "known associates" was a Jack Foley whose date of birth and year in which he died was the same, though he died in Los Angeles. I had heard the term "foley" before. The mention of Los Angeles somehow knocked this knowledge loose. How many films had I seen with "foley artists" in the credits? How could I be so obtuse, when Foley himself had practically beat me over the head with this information? Adding sound effects to film by, say, approximating a punch to the gut by hitting a side of beef with a baseball bat, squishing hand soap for the sound of boots in mud, manipulating cellophane to evoke a crackling fire, grinding a pistachio nut into a metal surface to achieve the sound of a human skull being crushed, running a handheld fan for the sound of a giant hovering dragonfly, the sound of armored soldiers marching achieved by jangling keys, watermelons and unripe coconuts chopped in half to approximate decapitation.

Was this an error in the record, or were Jack Foley

and Foley Senior one and the same? Were they brothers somehow born the same year, half-brothers, were they twins? Was Donovan Foley, my Donovan Foley, actually the son or nephew of the person responsible for pioneering manual sound effects in a nascent film industry? Other options presented themselves but seemed absurd enough to be out of bounds.

<h1 style="text-align:center">33</h1>

What I didn't foresee was remaining in Bevacqua's mansion for days, in a kind of fog. I arranged for the other manager to cover me at Shred Authority Neighborhood Storage. Though I didn't eat much, I took Bevacqua up on his suggestion to microwave some of the food in his freezer. I drank filtered water and performed calisthenics to clear my head. He was even kind enough to lead me to a room on the second floor, what looked like a child's room with a nautical theme, where he invited me to sleep when I wanted, offered the use of a full bath down the hall.

"I've had my best maid go over it with bleach, for your peace of mind," he said. He handed me a towel and a pair of flip-flops, wrapped in plastic.

"Shower shoes. Unopened," he said.

I rarely saw Bevacqua during my stay, rarely heard a sound except the house settling, except for soft footsteps late one night that made me think of Blanche. I availed myself of a dusty liquor cabinet off the library: the Scotch was fine, other spirits did their job, though some of the liqueur had become solid after many years.

I watched feeds for hours at a time, jumping from known associate to known associate. My celebrity and personal curiosity were quickly exhausted. I found a website frequented by those with access to the Utah Data Center on which they shared and sometimes traded footage of interest. This was nothing official, a hidden wiki inside a hidden wiki maintained by anonymous data analysts, IT specialists, systems administrators, government contractors, and who knew what else.

In this flourishing ecosystem of images, the photos and videos considered most engaging rose to the top. Some had hundreds or thousands of comments. In this way, the site resembled other legitimate aggregator and discussion sites, except all the media on this one had been gathered surreptitiously.

The logic of the Internet extended to its deepest parts. I felt both attracted and repulsed, and eventually felt ill, having seen images that would linger in my memory until death, most likely. I left the aggregation of illicit media, and tried and failed to find Bevacqua's medical records somewhere on the 96% of the Deep Web that wasn't indexed. Poking around in the dark, I found sites for weapons, drugs, illegal porn, bank details for sale, contract killing offers. I went back to hopping from known associate to known associate, limiting the field corresponding to my own geographic area. The faces I cycled through were normal enough, family member after family member, loner to shut-in to woman about town. I observed dozens, hundreds of city dwellers going about their business, sleeping, enjoying a private moment. The experience again reminded me of the Internet, in particular of the once-popular video chat website that randomly paired one user with another user elsewhere in the world via webcam. Each concept was unhealthy in its own way. After a period of particularly mundane feeds, and when I had nearly decided to return to work, return home, go anywhere else, something gripped me from the screen.

The footage was of a man alone in a bedroom. He was older, well dressed in a gray suit, graying hair. Though completely visible and in focus, unlike some of us, the man was a kind of gray spot. He appeared to be the kind of older man who took care of his appearance. He bent over a desk, a shaded lamp with a green shade its only ornament. What caught my eye was the bed, or what was on it: piles and stacks of American currency.

Until this point I hadn't considered the utility of the surveillance system with regard to profit, that is to say with regard to theft of some sort. This newfound interest, I told myself, was strictly academic. I zoomed out to ascertain the man's address, returned to the bedroom view. He approached a walk-in closet, turned on a light, and approached the gray panel of a fuse box. After fiddling with the panel, it swung open to reveal a safe with a combination lock. Perhaps ironically, the cameras in this man's apartment allowed for multiple viewing angles, including one providing me with the combination. The man took trips from bed to closet, carefully arranging stacks of cash, sliding them into the back of the safe. He paused from time to time, hefting a stack, thumbing it, fanning his withered face. Once the safe was filled and the bed cleared, he lay down to nap.

I researched the man, found out he was married—no children. At the moment, his wife was at work in a nearby high-rise. He was technically retired, received monthly payments from the federal government, and was involved in some heavy illegal activities. The apartment building, I learned, was guarded, but not by your usual doorman-type security. It was monitored by an increasingly common (and more cost-effective) remote service in which security company employees monitored multiple buildings on plasma screens, opening doors for familiar residents who had forgotten their fob, allowing mail carriers entry to leave packages in a secure space, and locking the entire building down in case of any funny business. The system employed face-recognition software that allowed the authorized to come and go without pause.

Presented with the idea of a pile of money, I dreamed up ways to gain entry while the apartment was vacant. I was confident I could use Bevacqua's access to somehow disable the remote monitoring. It also occurred to me that Foley, using his particular abilities, would be able to enter the building without a hitch.

This particular apartment, I decided, was a bit of a hard target, and there was no need to take unnecessary risks. I returned to the dark net markets and ordered ketamine, DMT, and MDMA, having them shipped to Shred Authority under my name, and paying for them with untraceable digital cryptocurrency. One might rightly ask why I had the drugs shipped to me in my name, and the answer is simple: if you receive a parcel of some illegal substance, and the authorities can prove you requested its delivery, it doesn't matter whose name is on the mailing label. Ergo, it's safer to have the parcel addressed to yourself. Especially since the United States Postal Service keeps detailed records on the individuals receiving mail at any given address, and the sudden appearance of mail to an unfamiliar name amounts to a red flag—both for the post office and your usual mail carrier.

After making the purchase, an idea began to form. I went to the part of the dark net where one acquired untraceable digital currency—bitcoin, and other varieties. One common method was to make a bank transfer to a cryptocurrency service, who would then release an equivalent amount of digital funds. I ruled this out since my identity would be tied to the original transaction. Anti-money laundering laws required official exchanges selling untraceable currency to record your legal name and some other proof of identity, thus undoing the utility of the cryptocurrency in the first place. A slightly more secure option would be to visit one of several cryptocurrency ATMs throughout the city. They were the reverse of your traditional ATM in that you inserted cash, and in turn were credited with funds in your digital wallet. My sense in this case was that the ATMs were surely surveilled, which I was able to confirm in short order. These cryptocurrencies weren't illegal, though if you planned to use them for illegal activities, it was best to leave no trail, which is why I decided to arrange a few in-person meetings with so-called crypto-hustlers.

<h1 style="text-align:center">34</h1>

The first crypto-hustler wanted to meet at a busy chain coffeehouse during the lunch rush. I arrived early, ordered a coffee, paid with cash, and hovered until a table opened up with a view of the door. We had established a time, but no mention was made of how to identify one another. I scrutinized each person who arrived alone, rejecting a series of customers as the potential seller for being too clean-cut, or too old, or too square, or too business casual, or too slow, or too young, or too bubbly. A man in a jean jacket who looked just the right age made eye contact with me, and I knew this was my guy. I nearly spoke when he walked past, making a beeline for the cashier. I was getting ready to leave when nearly ten minutes after our meeting time another prospect entered the café. He scanned the room, seemed to consider one solitary man in the corner, noticed me, and approached. He was roughly my age, and wearing jeans, sneakers, gray hoodie, glasses with thick frames, and a black and gunmetal laptop bag.

"We have a meeting?" he said, sitting down.

"Yes. CoinBlaster?"

"Yes," he said. "HeadWoundGuy99?"

We both laughed, establishing a rapport that would make my eventual aim more difficult to carry out. I was wearing a fake mustache that I feared could be blown off by the force of my exhalations.

"So you wanted seventy-five," he said.

I nodded. I had decided on this increment since it was

a sizable amount that fell short of one hundred dollars, which seemed to me a tipping point of sorts. Many have been robbed for far less than seventy-five dollars, I knew, but the temptation increased when a third digit came into play.

"Should I put it on the table?" I asked.

The hustler's look suggested his realization that this was my first time. He pulled out his phone.

"Sure," he said. "You can count it in front of you, and open your wallet program."

I placed a twenty, a twenty, a twenty, a ten, and a five on the café table, then folded all in half to reduce the visible surface area. I resolved to bump up the amount to eighty for my next transaction, so as to simplify the process and reduce the number of bills by one.

The hustler asked for the code corresponding to my digital wallet, which I conveyed. He then showed me the screen on his phone, featuring my wallet's code and the amount of $75.00.

"OK. You can place it in front of me, and I'll hit submit."

After the transaction cleared, which happened instantly as far as I could tell, he flashed the thumbs-up, grinned, pocketed the money, and was gone.

35

I upped the next exchange to $200.00, bringing along two crisp one hundred-dollar bills. The crypto-hustler's username, which played a large part in my establishing contact, was filmfanatic5. Like his predecessor, this hustler had picked a busy café for our meeting. He had requested, for purposes of identification, that I purchase a package of sticky nametag labels from an office supply store and affix one to my breast. He said it didn't matter if I wrote a name there, so I chose to leave it blank.

I failed to notice the man when he entered, or perhaps my eyes passed over him without registering his presence. My first awareness occurred as he entered my field of vision from behind, approaching the vacant seat at my table with coffee in hand. He was wearing a suit, tie, and Jeffrey Dahmer glasses—large, thick, with silver frames.

"Ted, great to see you. How are the wife and kids?"

The hustler reached across the table and shook my hand with enthusiasm, words tumbling faster than mere coffee might explain. His canned statement was a code we had agreed upon hours before.

"They're fantastic, Bill. Thanks for asking," I said.

Satisfied, the hustler leaned in to whisper:

"All right, let's do this. I have a plane to catch."

I slipped him the two crisp one hundred-dollar bills. The currency was brand new, with security features of such complexity and beauty as to constitute a work of art. Holding a note up to the light revealed hidden images and watermarks. From the blank space to the right of the bill's portrait emerged Benjamin Franklin's ghostly image, a kind of negative double. A blue, 3D security ribbon adorned the note as though conferring a prize. Tilting the note sideways caused images of bells woven into the paper to morph into dancing 100s; tilting it in another cardinal direction made the 100s and bells dance from side to side. Color-shifting ink concealed a bell within the illustration of an inkwell, which was either green or copper-colored, depending on the angle. A security thread imprinted with three letters—U, S, and A—would glow pink when exposed to ultraviolet light. On the genuine article, Franklin's left shoulder felt rough to the touch, a result of a process called "raised printing." Close attention to Franklin's jacket collar revealed tiny printed text, i.e. "microprinting," that read "THE UNITED STATES OF AMERICA." Microprinting around the invisible watermark read "USA 100," and along the golden quill, that wondrous implement of inscription, one could find "ONE HUNDRED USA." Elsewhere, image shifted to reveal text, and text shifted to reveal image. Like a print by Dürer, this object was the end result of the intaglio process—truly a work of art.

The hustler took out a counterfeit pen, marking on the corner of each bill. This left the usual mark—yellow to colorless—rather than the dark one that would appear on something made of paper rather than fiber. He held the bills up to the light for good measure.

36

My next rendezvous to convert cash to digital currency was to take place in an after-work watering hole below street level. I brought $400 in hundreds this time, my rationale being that this amount would be less of a temptation to potential rip-off artists than, say, $500. I also wanted to conduct business with a higher level of entrepreneur, for reasons I'll explain. The bar was a "shotgun" layout, straight back to a bathroom I never entered. I sat and ordered a beer to occupy myself, nervous that my decision-making abilities were taking a hit, though unable to do otherwise.

The individual I was meeting went by the username of cuLtLeader, something I could have attributed meaning to but somehow didn't. He had a "reputation score" of 99, after all.

Nearly finished with my beer, I gave the rest of the crowded bar another look. Three young men whose appearance suggested they'd be legally barred from entry clustered around a circular high top. I approached and placed my glass on the table. If forced to guess, I'd say the youngest of the three was a senior in high school, the next was 20 max, and the third could've been the cooler older brother of either one. He was wearing a baseball cap with the logo of the Tokyo Yomiuri Giants.

"You're the guy," he said.

"Yeah."

"You off the grid?"

"No," I said. "Why?"

"A lot of my customers are," he said. "Libertarians."

His friends, relatives, or friend and relative laughed.

"Sorry I brought people along," he said.

"It's no problem," I said.

I said I needed to close my tab at the bar. When I came back, all three had phones in hand. Every hustler I had encountered so far was wearing a backpack, I realized. I asked the kid if he was ready, gave him the 34 digits that would point him to my digital wallet, handed over the cash, and watched the transfer go through.

The youngest of the three pointed at my beer glass on the edge of the table.

"You shouldn't leave your drink unattended, you know," he said.

37

I cycled through users like MasterCleanse, hiddenlevel, Beezelbub3, thefriendliest, springheeled, IdahoBro4, and HiGHeRSOURCe. I drained my bank account, initiated several large cash advances, applied for additional lines of credit and maxed them out. I divided the money into piles of $800, reasoning that the temptation to rob would be less than if I went for an amount with four digits, and set up meetings with a series of crypto-hustlers until I had a sizable digital nest egg and a deep roster to draw from. I wasn't robbed even once, and only once was I on the receiving end of a scam: a twitchy individual somehow reversed the transaction after I was out of sight, or he managed to send me fake confirmation. A small price to pay. The last transaction, or the penultimate one if you looked at it a certain way, oddly enough took place in the parking lot of a police station. The hustler I met there told me it was for his protection, and mine.

This last hustler was wearing a t-shirt printed with the entire script to *Hackers* (1995) in very small letters, which for some reason made me think fondly of Bevacqua. Here I was, a paper shredder dipping his toe in the world of the digital, the shredding facility employee chasing the image maker. Text pursuing image.

The next phase was to review the footage of each of my transactions, identify the hustlers I had met, and determine, if not where they lived, then where they kept their cash. I only needed one subject; it would be a simple affair by design. Using the link to the Utah data center, I researched each slinger of digital currency. A fair number owned a firearm, which immediately ruled them out. Ditto those who lived in buildings with heavy security. Those who lived alone were more appealing, though roommates were not a deal-breaker, necessarily.

Among those who remained, I observed their movements, associates, and the size of their stash. My subject became manifest. He lived alone on the second floor of a duplex, partied on the weekends and during the week, sold bitcoin and medical grade cannabis, and had a startling amount of cash secreted throughout his house: sewn into couch cushions, in ziplock bags in the toilet tank, in the freezer, in a safe, under floorboards, in a file cabinet, in a sleeping bag stuff sack on a closet's top shelf. Things I could do with this amount of money: erase my debt, live comfortably for a couple years or frugally for several, finance a computer science degree from the Utah community college of my choosing. There would be money left over. In terms of guilt concerning the hustler I was about to rob, I had none. I knew he would recover.

I considered, at length, the number of wrongs I had committed since reaching puberty—the laws broken, trusts betrayed, the expectations I had failed to meet— and decided what I was about to do was on the low end of the transgression spectrum.

Using footage from cameras within the hustler's pad and the surrounding streets, I settled on a route approaching the apartment via a quiet side avenue, a method of entry, a nondescript gym bag to fill with cash, an exit route, and a separate side street leading to another sleepy neighborhood. Armed with foreknowledge of various kinds, including the knowledge that the subject was at a bar three miles away and would remain there, should past habit be any indication, for at least the next four hours, I entered the subject's back yard via a locked gate that could be opened by inserting a hand between the bars and turning a deadbolt. I retrieved a ladder leaning against a shed, leaned it against the duplex—the subject's downstairs neighbors were also at a distant bar—and opened the window I knew to be unlocked and without a screen. After entering the window and closing it behind me, my next move was to immediately leave the apartment in the standard manner and return the ladder to its place, so as to minimize the time in which a ladder might be seen leaning against the structure. I went back inside, locked the back door, located the gym bag I had noticed earlier, loaded it with cash, and left the apartment via the front door. Though the deadbolt was impossible for me to lock behind myself, this was hardly evidence of a break-in, as it was the same door the subject had last used and one might assume he had forgotten to lock it after leaving. The building's front door locked automatically behind me, and the subject's apartment was exactly how he had left it, except for the unlocked inner door, missing cash, missing bag. Not that evidence mattered a great deal, since drug dealers, like militant defenders of the Second Amendment, tend to avoid dialing 911. All told, I was inside for ten minutes, tops, less time than takes to pack.

I had of course been wearing gloves—gray, powder free, latex ones purchased with cash. Miles later, I placed them in a shopping bag and tossed the ball of plastic into a trash can. After returning home with the cash, I stepped out again, and disposed of the gym bag in a faraway receptacle. The bag itself was unremarkable.

38

The next morning I stopped by the Shred Authority office to gather some items of value. In the bathroom, I noticed a poster taped to the door. It reminded me of a vision chart, except instead of letters, it featured progressively smaller rows of a broken circle in various configurations, a symbol like an altered letter "C":

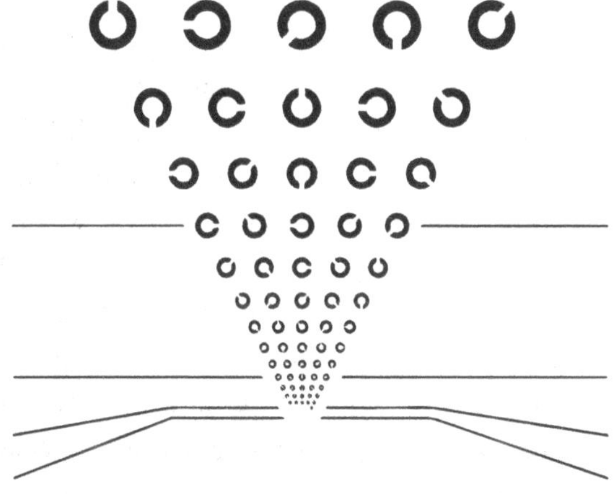

Research revealed this was indeed a vision chart, of the logarithmic variety. Not only could the chart be used to test the visual acuity of someone who couldn't read, but the test was more accurate than a linguistic one. The human subject, apparently, was surprisingly adept at recognizing blurry letters, as opposed to mere shapes. In other words, we can often read something that is nearly invisible. The way the chart worked was thus: the patient would be asked to look at a certain line and state where the gap in the symbol appeared, i.e., left, right, up, down, or any of the remaining 45 degree positions. The patient would continue until unable to determine where the gaps fell, which is to say until unable to distinguish a broken circle from a complete one. The symbol in question had a number of names, including the Landolt ring, Landolt C, Landolt circle, and Landolt broken ring. It is named after Edmund Landolt, a pupil of Herman Snellen, the ophthalmologist who developed the ubiquitous Snellen chart.

I peeled the poster off the door and fed it into a shredder, relishing the further breakdown of already fragmented images. I shredded the chart and felt immense, vertiginous pleasure course through my body. Shredding fulfilled me, I realized, and Bevacqua's films had ended up filling a gap that was an inverse of this desire. The same was true for watching faraway strangers' faces on screen. The thing I loved about film itself was the thing I loved to an even greater degree in the films of Lucian Bevacqua. When you're reading a book, you can put it down; you can stop reading. But when you're watching a film, especially in the theater, there's no pause—there's no way out. The film keeps flowing and passing over you, unless you close your eyes, lose consciousness, or physically leave the space. This was true not only for the audience of Bevacqua's films, but for its very subjects. Once you're the star of a Bevacqua film, there's no way out.

It was inevitable that Donovan Foley's face, its blurriness, its illegibility, would come to mind. The gaps in the symbols on the vision chart corresponded to something missing from my vision, a piece of information just outside my reach. Foley was the star of an oeuvre so large that no one had seen it all, not even him. It was like America in that sense—you couldn't comprehend it in its totality. Only in pieces. Fragments. All along I had been viewing and collecting, searching for the Bevacqua film behind the Bevacqua film. The film that existed as the negative space surrounding all the fragments I had viewed and failed to find. But if somewhere out there was the film behind the film, what did the America behind the America look like? And the totality of its history? I called Foley for what I thought would be the final time.

We had a long conversation, or what I would consider long. It lasted an hour and fifteen minutes. The word "friendship," oddly enough, was used five times. Bevacqua's name was uttered at least sixteen times. The word "interstate" was said seven times. The word "blank" was said seven times. The word _____ as well. Blanche's name came up nineteen times. The word "film" was spoken forty times. The word "evil," I supposed, was said thirteen times. The word "voyeur" six times. The word "network" nineteen times. The word "screen" thirty-two times. The word "loneliness" five times. The word "cult" three times. The word "letter" seventeen times. The word "America" came up one time. The word "sex" was spoken. The word "text" six times. The word "love" was spoken three times. The word "signifier" twelve times. The word "highway" occurred twice. The word "Chile" once. The word "image" thirty-five times. The word "sound" fourteen times. The word "death" numerous times. The word "killer" eighteen times. The word "empty" twenty-one times. The word "celluloid" and the word "grain" occurred.

I took the bus to Hertz. Using one of ten driver's licenses I had purchased online, each featuring my photograph and one of ten aliases, I selected the vehicle with the most autonomous features they had on offer—it was an E-Class.

Abridged contents of the car, including trunk, backseat, and backpack buckled into passenger seat:

Protein bars (2)

Pistol

Assorted stimulants (pills, powder)

Books (3): Hollywood Lighting from the Silent Era to Film Noir; Tome of Terror: Horror Films of the Silent Era; Silent Lives: 100 Biographies of the Silent Film Era

1-Gallon water jugs (4 [2 full, 2 empty])

Cash (assorted bills)

US Road Atlas

Condoms (1 package)

Utah State Map

I drove west, or rode west, depending on your definition, for 20 hours, maybe 30. Nodding off was inevitable, despite dipping into my bag every hour or so. The car's Drive Pilot feature as part of the Driver Assistance package kept me on the road, in my lane, and at safe distances from other vehicles.

By the time I reached Utah, I had nearly emptied one of the water jugs, and had made considerable progress toward filling another. Utah, home to the Intelligence Community Comprehensive National Cybersecurity Initiative Data Center, containing data amounting to a record of every phone call, text message, Internet search, purchase, and keystroke executed in the United States, home to the site of America as text, radiated a strange energy that filled the car as soon as it crossed the border. White salt in every direction, a vast blankness. I had a destination in mind, but no real goal, at least none that I had articulated consciously. I didn't foresee a pressing need for the pistol or for the condoms—far more likely, I supposed, that I'd use either on myself.

When the low-fuel warning chime sounded, I instructed the car to leave the highway and find the nearest gas station. The car was as of yet unable to refuel itself, so I went inside to prepay with cash. All I had eaten in roughly 24 hours was the pair of protein bars, more of which caught my eye in the station. I started to grab a few of the chocolate variety, then decided to pick up the whole box and take it to the cashier. I counted nine bars remaining in the box.

"Hello," I said. "I'd like the rest on pump three, please."

"We don't sell those by the box," he said, looking at the protein bars.

"Oh, sorry. I just picked it up to carry the bars. There are nine in there."

The cashier picked up the box and scanned the barcode on the outside.

"Fifteen fifty-three, and the rest on gas," he said, taking the fifty-dollar bill out of my grasp.

"There are only nine in there," I said.

"You want the box or not?"

"You can keep the box. I just want the bars. Anyway, I think they're two for three."

"OK, let me void this," he said.

The cashier dumped the bars on the counter, counted

aloud to nine, and scanned each one individually. He made a neat pile next to the empty box.

"Have you been working here long?" I asked.

"Do you want a bag?"

I stood in the desert heat until the tank was full.

I never had a master plan, or any other kind of plan, really. I had merely embarked upon a course of action whose every contour pushed me forward in a way I couldn't control. The interstate cut through desert and low mountain terrain. I pissed on the way to Salt Lake City, tossed the jug out the window, and instructed the car to take U.S. Route 15 south as the sun went down.

The vehicle moved through grids of its own accord, passing exits for places called White City, Jordan, West Jordan, Sandy, Desiccation Station, and so on. When the road lacked a center divider, I could only instruct the car to exceed the speed limit by five miles per hour. On the highway, I was capped at 90. As a place called Bluffdale approached, I set the speed at fourteen over, nine over. I turned down the radio, then silenced it. The number of official vehicles soon outnumbered apparent civilians on the road. I tried to find a radio station with a human voice, some piece of linguistic data on which I could concentrate in the desert void.

The car approached a ring road, one that I knew encircled two more. This outer ring featured gas stations and other public amenities, and was likely the border beyond which suspicion was easily aroused. Somewhere within these loops was the massive data center: locus of so much, a dark body with an invisible interior that would continue to grow without changing size. I instructed the car to take a left, choosing to begin the circuit—clockwise—that seemed most logical. A surge of panic passed through my nervous system as I realized I had never touched a ukulele.

The ring road was only a ring road in name—it certainly was a road, though its ring consisted of a kind of loose square with rounded edges. I instructed the vehicle to avoid all exits, told it to change lanes when the words "EXIT ONLY" appeared. When our entry point to the beltway appeared again, at the northern tip of the loop, I instructed the car to head southeast, remaining in the circuit. I considered my path's relation to the broken circles of the vision chart. The gaps in the loop of the ring road were visible, though how many actual breaks in the loop existed was an open question.

I observed what I thought was sagebrush, illuminated by yellow arc-sodiums in the near-dusk. Wind rocked the vehicle. I thought about the "switches," one or two dozen throughout the U.S., large structures with no windows at key nodes and transit points for all the data headed to Utah. I thought about satellites, about web traffic passing through cables, about collection, about the ability to search by term, phrase, name, address, travel destination, financial transaction, and so on. I felt content sitting in the car, safe because the facility was not yet visible. I also felt safe, having read that Utah was the sixth-safest U.S. state, in terms of road safety, climatic disasters, workplace safety, crime, and financial security.

After completing a second lap, I instructed the vehicle to continue, finding a command called "repeat route." I felt content. The highway, part of our critical infrastructure, was also close to one of the Internet's so-called "backbones." The speed of light in a fiber optic cable was only about 1/3 the speed of light in a vacuum, I had recently learned. The car, of its own accord, completed a third lap. I felt a sense of fulfillment so long absent as to be nearly alien. I had no need to urinate, wasn't thirsty or hungry, and the means to satisfy these needs was present. Powder from a plastic bag to my damp fingertip to my tongue was the source of roughly half the euphoria I experienced. Gas, perhaps, would be an issue, but not for a considerable time. I was closing in on something central, or, failing that, something containing an answer to whatever I was seeking. Whether I learned the answer didn't even matter, what mattered was being close to a place containing all the answers. All I had to do was continue. I was closing in, but I had the sense that I could leave at any time, could take any of several centrifugal routes out—visible or invisible gaps or breaches. I became pleasantly conscious of my body sinking into the reclining seat. It wouldn't make a difference whether I was asleep or awake for whatever was to come. On what must have been the seventh lap, a helicopter appeared—silent, floating out of the pixelated night.

My thanks to everyone for advice, critique, and close reading, especially Cris Mazza, Christopher Grimes, Rick Moody, Walter Benn Michaels, Joseph Tabbi, Luis Urrea, Jac Jemc, Michael Kimball, Amy Wallen, and Gordon Lish. Many thanks to friends, colleagues, and students in the English Department at the University of Illinois at Chicago, and to those who engaged with these pages during workshops and colloquia. I'm grateful to Robert Boyers and the New York State Summer Writers Institute at Skidmore College for generous support and literary community.

Thank you to the editors of journals in which the following excerpts appeared: "Schrödinger's Bullet" in *Green Mountains Review*, ed. Jensen Beach; "Items for Sleeping and Lying" in *Subtropics*, ed. David Leavitt; "Karst System" in *Your Impossible Voice*, ed. Stephen Beachy. My gratitude to TT, Aurelia, and Spuyten Duyvil Publishing.

For encouragement and a great deal else, special thanks to my parents. Thank you to my friends and family—literal and adopted, IRL and online.

Brooks Sterritt is Assistant Professor of English at the University of Houston-Victoria. A former Fulbright Scholar to Germany, his writing has appeared in *The Nation*, *The New Republic*, *The Believer*, *Subtropics*, and elsewhere. *The History of America in My Lifetime* is his first novel.